Adeline Dutton Train Whitney

A summer in Leslie Goldthwaite's life

Adeline Dutton Train Whitney

A summer in Leslie Goldthwaite's life

ISBN/EAN: 9783743301306

Manufactured in Europe, USA, Canada, Australia, Japa

Cover: Foto ©ninafisch / pixelio.de

Manufactured and distributed by brebook publishing software
(www.brebook.com)

Adeline Dutton Train Whitney

A summer in Leslie Goldthwaite's life

To the Memory

OF

MY DEAR FRIEND

MARIA S. CUMMINS,

AND

OF DAYS AMONG THE MOUNTAINS MADE BEAUTIFUL
BY HER COMPANIONSHIP,

I DEDICATE

THIS LITTLE STORY.

A SUMMER IN LESLIE GOLDTHWAITE'S LIFE.

I.

"NOTHING but leaves — leaves — leaves ! The green things don't know enough to do anything better ! "

Leslie Goldthwaite said this, standing in the bay-window among her plants, which had been green and flourishing, but persistently blossomless, all winter, and now the spring days were come.

Cousin Delight looked up ; and her white ruffling, that she was daintily hemstitching, fell to her lap, as she looked, still with a certain wide intentness in her eyes, upon the pleasant window, and the bright, fresh things it framed. Not the least bright and fresh among them was the human creature in her early girlhood, tender and pleasant in its beautiful leafage, but waiting, like any other young and growing life, to prove what sort of flower should come of it.

" Now you 've got one of your ' thoughts,' Cousin Delight! I see it ' biggening,' as Elspie says." Leslie turned round, with her little green watering-pot suspended in her hand, waiting for the thought.

To have a thought, and to give it, were nearly simultaneous things with Cousin Delight ; so true, so pure, so unselfish, so made to give, — like perfume or music, which cannot be, and be withheld, — were thoughts with her.

1 must say a word, before I go further, of Delight Goldthwaite. I think of her as of quite a young person ; you, youthful readers, would doubtless have declared that she was old, — very old, at least for a young lady. She was twenty-eight, at this time of which I write; Leslie, her young cousin, was just "past the half, and catching up," as she said herself, — being fifteen. Leslie's mother called Miss Goldthwaite, playfully, "Ladies' Delight"; and, taking up the idea, half her women-friends knew her by this significant and epigrammatic title. There was something doubly pertinent in it. She made you think, at once, of nothing so much as heart's-ease; a garden heart's-ease, — that flower of many names; not of the frail, scentless, wild wood-violet, — she had been cultured to something larger. The violet nature was there, colored and shaped more richly, and gifted with rare fragrance — for those whose delicate sense could perceive it. The very face was a pansy-face; with its deep, large, purple-blue eyes, and golden brows and lashes, the color of her hair, — pale gold, so pale that careless people who had perception only for such beauty as can flash upon you from a crowd, or across a drawing-room, said hastily that she had *no* brows or lashes, and that this spoiled her. She was not a beauty, therefore ; nor was she, in any sort, a belle. She never drew around her the common attention that is paid eagerly to very pretty, outwardly bewitching girls; and she never seemed to care for this. At a party, she was as apt as not to sit in a corner; but

the quiet people, — the mothers, looking on, or the girls, waiting for partners, — getting into that same corner also, found the best pleasure of their evening there. There was something about her dress, too, that women appreciated most fully; the delicate textures, — the finishings — and only those — of rare, exquisite lace, — the perfect harmony of the whole unobtrusive toilet, — women looked at these in wonder at the unerring instinct of her taste; in wonder, also, that they only with each other raved about her. Nobody had ever been supposed to be devoted to her; she had never been reported as " engaged "; there had never been any of this sort of gossip about her; gentlemen found her, they said, hard to get acquainted with; she had not much of the small talk which must usually begin an acquaintance; a few — her relatives, or her elders, or the husbands of her intimate married friends — understood and valued her; but it was her girl-friends and women-friends who knew her best, and declared that there was nobody like her; and so came her sobriquet, and the double pertinence of it.

Especially she was Leslie Goldthwaite's delight. Leslie had no sisters, and her aunts were old, — far older than her mother; on her father's side, a broken and scattered family had left few ties for her; next to her mother, and even closer, in some young sympathies, she clung to Cousin Delight.

With this diversion, we will go back, now, to her, and to her thought.

" I was thinking," she said, with that intent look in her eyes, " I often think, of how something else was found, once, having nothing but leaves; and of what came to it."

"I know," answered Leslie, with an evasive quickness, and turned round with her watering-pot to her plants again.

There was sometimes a bit of waywardness about Leslie Goldthwaite; there was a fitfulness of frankness and re-serve. She was eager for truth; yet now and then she would thrust it aside. She said that "nobody liked a nicely pointed moral better than she did; only she would just as lief it should n't be pointed at her." The fact was, she was in that sensitive state in which many a young girl finds herself, when she begins to ask and to weigh with herself the great questions of life, and shrinks shyly from the open mention of the very thing she longs more fully to apprehend.

Cousin Delight took no notice; it is, perhaps, likely that she understood sufficiently well for that. She turned toward the table by which she sat, and pulled towards her a heavy Atlas that lay open at the map of Connecticut. Beside it was Lippincott's Gazetteer, — open, also.

"Travelling, Leslie?"

"Yes. I 've been a charming journey this morning, before you came. I wonder if I ever *shall* travel, in reality. I 've done a monstrous deal of it with maps and gazetteers."

"This has n't been one of the stereotyped tours, it seems."

"O no! What 's the use of doing Niagara or the White Mountains, or even New York, and Philadelphia, and Washington, on the map? I 've been one of my little by-way trips; round among the villages; stopping wherever I found one cuddled in between a river and a

hill, or in a little sea-shore nook. Those are the places,
after all, that I would hunt out, if I had plenty of money
to go where I liked with. It's so pleasant to imagine
how the people live there, and what sort of folks they
would be likely to be. It is n't so much travelling as
living round, — awhile in one home, and then in another.
How many different little biding-places there are in the
world! And how queer it is only really to know about
one or two of them!"

"What's this place you're at just now? Winsted?"

"Yes; there's where I've brought up, at the end of
that bit of railroad. It's a bigger place than I fancied,
though. I always steer clear of the names that end in
'ville.' They're sure to be stupid, money-making
towns, all grown up in a minute, with some common
man's name tacked on to them, that happened to build a
saw-mill, or something, first. But Winsted has such a
sweet, little, quiet English sound. I know it never
began with a mill. They make pins and clocks and tools
and machines there now; and it's 'the largest and most
prosperous post-village of Litchfield County.' But I
don't care for the pins and machinery. It's got a lake
alongside of it; and Still River — don't that sound nice?
— runs through; and there are the great hills — big
enough to put on the map — out beyond. I can fancy
where the girls take their sunset walks; and the moonlight parties, boating on the pond, and the way the woods
look, round Still River. O yes! that's one of the
places I mean to go to."

Leslie Goldthwaite lived in one of the inland cities of
Massachusetts. She had grown up and gone to school

there, and had never yet been thirty miles away. Hei father was a busy lawyer, making a handsome living for his family, and laying aside abundantly for their future provision, but giving himself no lengthened recreations, and scarcely thinking of them as needful for the rest.

It was a pleasant, large, brown, wooden house they lived in, on the corner of two streets; with a great, green door-yard about it on two sides, where chestnut and cherry trees shaded it from the public way, and flower-beds brightened under the parlor windows, and about the porch. Just greenness and bloom enough to suggest, always, more; just sweetness and sunshine and bird-song enough, in the early summer days, to whisper of broad fields and deep woods where they rioted without stint; and these days always put Leslie into a certain happy impatience, and set her dreaming and imagining; and she learned a great deal of her geography in the fashion that we have hinted at.

Miss Goldthwaite was singularly discursive and frag- mentary in her conversation this morning, somehow. She dropped the map-travelling suddenly, and asked a new question. "And how comes on the linen-drawer?"

"O Cousin Del! I'm humiliated, — disgusted! I feel as small as butterflies' pinfeathers! I've been to see the Haddens. Mrs. Linceford has just got home from Paris, and brought them wardrobes to last to remotest posterity! And *such* things! Such rufflings, and stitchings, and embroiderings! Why, mine look — as if they'd been made by the blacksmith!"

The "linen-drawer" was an institution of Mrs. Gold- thwaite's; resultant, partly, from her old-fashioned New

that had already begun to make promise of filling a
drawer, which she drew out as she answered Cousin
Delight's question.

The fine-lined gathers; the tiny dots of stitches that
held them to their delicate bindings; the hems and tucks,
true to a thread, and dotted with the same fairy needle-
dimples; (no machine-work, but all real, dainty finger-
craft;) the bits of ruffling peeping out from the folds,
with their edges in almost invisible whip-hems; and here
and there a finishing of lovely, lace-like crochet, done at
odd minutes, and for "visiting-work";—there was something prettier and more precious, really, in all this, than in
the imported fineries which had come, without labor and
without thought, to her friends the Haddens. Besides,
there were the pleasant talks and readings of the winter
evenings, all threaded in and out, and associated indeli-
bly with every seam. There was the whole of David
Copperfield, and the beginning of Our Mutual Friend,
ruffled up into the night-dresses; and some of the crochet
was beautiful with the rhymed pathos of Enoch Arden,
and some with the poetry of the Wayside Inn; and there
were places where stitches had had to be picked out and
done over, when the eye grew dim and the hand trembled
while the great war-news was being read.

Leslie loved it, and had a pride in it all; it was not,
truly and only, humiliation and disgust at self-comparison
with the Haddens, but some other and unexplained doubt
which moved her now, and which was stirred often by this,
or any other of the objects and circumstances of her life,
and which kept her standing there with her hand upon
the bureau-knob, in a sort of absence, while Cousin Delight

looked in, approved, and presently dropped quietly, like a
bit of money into a contribution-box, the delicate breadths
of linen cambric she had finished hemstitching, and rolled
together among the rest.

"O, thank you! But, Cousin Delight," said Leslie,
shutting the drawer, and turning short round, suddenly,
"I wish you'd just tell me — what you think — is the
sense of that — about the fig-tree! I suppose it's awfully
wicked, but I never could see. Is everything fig-leaves
that is n't out and out fruit, and is it all to be cursed, and
why *should* there be anything but leaves when 'the time
of figs was not yet'?" After her first hesitation, she
spoke quickly, impetuously, and without pause, as something that *would* come out.

"I suppose that has troubled you, as I dare say it has
troubled a great many other people," said Cousin Delight.
"It used to be a puzzle and a trouble to me. But now it
seems to me one of the most beautiful things of all."
She paused.

"I can *not* see how," said Leslie, emphatically. "It
always seems to me so — somehow — unreasonable; and
— angry."

She said this in a lower tone, as afraid of the uttered
audacity of her own thought; and she walked off, as she
spoke, toward the window once more, and stood with her
back to Miss Goldthwaite, almost as if she wished to have
done, again, with the topic. It was not easy for Leslie to
speak out upon such things; it almost made her feel cross
when she had done it.

"People mistake the true cause and effect, I think,"
said Delight Goldthwaite, "and so lose all the wonderful

1 *

enforcement of that acted parable. It was not, 'Cursed be the fig-tree because I have found nothing thereon'; but. 'Let *no fruit* grow on thee, henceforward, forever.' It seems to me I can hear the tone of tender solemnity in which Jesus would say such words ; knowing, as only he knew, all that they meant, and what should come, inevitably, of such a sentence. 'And presently the fig-tree withered away.' The life was nothing, any longer, from the moment when it might not be, what all life is, a reaching forward to the perfecting of some fruit. There was nothing to come, ever again, of all its greenness and beauty, and the greenness and beauty, which were only a form and a promise, ceased to be. It was the way he took to show his disciples, in a manner they should never forget, the inexorable condition upon which all life is given, and that the barren life, so soon as its barrenness is absolutely hopeless, becomes a literal death."

Leslie stood still, with her back to Miss Goldthwaite, and her face to the window. Her perplexity was changed, but hardly cleared. There were many things that crowded into her thoughts, and might have been spoken ; but it was quite impossible for her to speak. Impossible on this topic, and she certainly could not speak, at once, on any other.

Many seconds of silence counted themselves between the two. Then Cousin Delight, feeling an intuition or much that held and hindered the young girl, spoke again. " Does this make life seem hard ? "

" Yes," said Leslie, then, with an effort that hoarsened her very voice, " frightful." And as she spoke, she turned again quickly, as if to be motionless longer were

to invite more talk, and went over to the other window,
where her bird-cage hung, and began to take down the
glasses.

"Like all parables, it is manifold," said Delight, gently. "There is a great hope in it, too."

Leslie was at her basin, now, turning the water-faucet,
to rinse and refill the little drinking-vessel. She handled
the things quietly, but she made no pause.

"It shows that, while we see the leaf, we may have
hope of the fruit, — in ourselves, or in others."

She could not see Leslie's face. If she had, she would
have perceived a quick lifting and lightening upon it.
Then, a questioning that would not very long be repressed to silence.

The glasses were put in the cage again, and presently
Leslie came back to a little low seat by Miss Goldthwaite's side, which she had been occupying before all
this talk began. "Other people puzzle me as much as myself," she said. "I think the whole world is running to
leaves, sometimes."

"Some things flower almost invisibly, and hide away
their fruit under thick foliage. It is often only when the
winds shake their leaves down, and strip the branches
bare, that we find the best that has been growing."

"They make a great fuss and flourish with the leaves,
though, as long as they can. And it's who shall grow the
broadest and tallest, and flaunt out with the most of them.
After all, it's natural; and they *are* beautiful, in themselves.
And there's a 'time' for leaves, too, before the figs."

"Exactly. We have a right to look for the leaves,
and to be glad of them. That is a part of the parable."

"Cousin Delight! Let's talk of real things, and let the parable alone a minute."

Leslie sprang, impulsively, to her bureau, again, and flung forth the linen-drawer.

"There are my fig-leaves, — some of them, — and here are more." She turned, with a quick movement, to her wardrobe; pulled out and uncovered a bonnet-box which held a dainty headgear of the new spring fashion, and then took down from a hook and tossed upon it a silken garment that fluttered with fresh ribbons. "How much of this outside business is right, and how much wrong, I should be glad to know? It all takes time and thoughts; and those are life. How much life must go into the leaves? That's what puzzles me. I can't do without the things; and I can't be let to take 'clear comfort' in them, as grandma says, either." She was on the floor, now, beside her little fineries; her hands clasped together about one knee, and her face turned up to Cousin Delight's. She looked as if she half believed herself to be ill used.

"And clothes are but the first want, — the primitive fig-leaves; the world is full of other outside business, — as much. outside as these," pursued Miss Goldthwaite, thoughtfully. "Everything is outside. Learning, and behaving, and going, and doing, and seeing, and hearing, and having. 'It's all a muddle,' as the poor man says in Hard Times."

"I don't think I can do without the parable," said Cousin Delight. "The real inward principle of the tree — that which corresponds to thought and purpose in the soul — urges always to the finishing of its life in the fruit.

The leaves are only by the way, — an outgrowth of the same vitality, and a process toward the end ; but never, in any living thing, the end itself."

" Um," said Leslie, in her nonchalant fashion again ; her chin between her two hands now, and her head making little appreciative nods. " That 's like condensed milk ; a great deal in a little of it. I 'll put the fig-leaves away now, and think it over."

But, as she sprang up, and came round behind Miss Goldthwaite's chair, she stopped and gave her a little kiss on the top of her head. If Cousin Delight had seen, there was a bright softness in the eyes, which told of feeling, and of gladness that welcomed the quick touch of truth.

Miss Goldthwaite knew one good thing, — when she had driven her nail. " She never hammered in the head with a punch, like a carpenter," Leslie said of her. She believed that, in moral tool-craft, that finishing imple-ment belonged properly to the hand of an after-work-man.

II.

I HAVE mentioned one little theory, relating solely to domestic thrift, which guided Mrs. Goldthwaite in her arrangements for her daughter. I believe that, with this exception, she brought up her family very nearly without any theory whatever. She did it very much on the taking-for-granted system. She took for granted that her children were born with the same natural perceptions as herself; that they could recognize, little by little, as they grew into it, the principles of the moral world, — reason, right, propriety, — as they recognized, growing into them, the conditions of their outward living. She made her own life a consistent recognition of these, and she lived *openly* before them. There was never any course pursued with sole calculation as to its effect on the children. Family discussion and deliberation was seldom with closed doors. Questions that came up were considered as they came ; and the young members of the household perceived as soon as their elders the "reasons why" of most decisions. They were part and parcel of the whole *régime*. They learned politeness by being as politely attended to as company. They learned to be reasonable by seeing how the *reason* compelled father and mother, and not by having their vision stopped short at the arbitrary fact that father and mother compelled them. I think, on the whole, the Goldthwaite no-method turned out as good a method as any. Men have found out lately that horses even may be guided without reins.

It was characteristic, therefore, that Mrs. Goldthwaite —
receiving one day a confidential note proposing to her a
pleasant plan in behalf of Leslie, and intended to guard
against a premature delight and eagerness, and so perhaps
an ultimate disappointment for that young lady — should
instantly, on reading it, lay it open upon the table before
her daughter. "From Mrs. Linceford," she said, "and
concerning you."

Leslie took it up, expecting, possibly, an invitation to
tea. When she saw what it really was, her dark eyes
almost blazed with sudden, joyous excitement.

"Of course, I should be delighted to say yes for you,"
said Mrs. Goldthwaite, "but there are things to be considered. I can't tell how it will strike your father."

"School," suggested Leslie, the light in her eyes quiet-
ing a little.

"Yes, and expense; though I don't think he would
refuse on that score. I should have *liked*" — Mrs. Goldthwaite's tone was only half, and very gently, objecting;
there was an inflection of ready self-relinquishment in it
also — "to have had your *first* journey with me. But
you might have waited a long time for that."

If Leslie were disappointed in the end, she would have
known that her mother's heart had been with her from
the beginning, and grown people seldom realize how this
helps even the merest child to bear a denial.

"There is only a month now to vacation," said the
young girl.

"What do you think Mr. Waylie would say?"

"I really think," answered Leslie, after a pause, "that
he would say it was better than books."

They sat at their sewing together, after this, without speaking very much more, at the present time, about it. Mrs. Goldthwaite was thinking it over in her motherly mind, and in the mind of Leslie thought and hope and anticipation were dancing a reel with each other. It is time to tell the reader of the what and why.

Mrs. Linceford, the elder married daughter of the Hadden family, — many years the elder of her sisters, Jeannie and Elinor, — was about to take them, under her care, to the mountains for the summer, and she kindly proposed joining Leslie Goldthwaite to her charge. "The Mountains" in New England means always, in common speech, the one royal range of the White Hills. ·

You can think what this opportunity was to a young girl full of fancy, loving to hunt out, even by map and gazetteer, the by-nooks of travel, and wondering already if she should ever really journey otherwise. You can think how she waited, trying to believe she could bear any decision, for the final determination concerning her.

"If it had been to Newport or Saratoga, I should have said no at once," said Mr. Goldthwaite. "Mrs. Linceford is a gay, extravagant woman, and the Haddens' ideas don't precisely suit mine. But the mountains, — she can't get into much harm there."

"I should n't have cared for Newport, or the Springs, father, truly," said Leslie, with a little hopeful flutter of eagerness in her voice, "but the real mountains, — O father !"

The " O father!" was not without its weight. Also Mr. Waylie, whom Mr. Goldthwaite called on and con

sulted, threw his opinion into the favoring scale, precisely
as Leslie had foreseen. He was a teacher who did not
imagine all possible educational advantage to be shut up
within the four walls of his or any other school-room.
"She is just the girl to whom it will do great good," he
said. Leslie's last week's lessons were not accomplished
the less satisfactorily for this word of his, and the pleasure
it opened to her.

There came a few busy days of stitching and starching,
and crimping and packing, and then, in the last of June,
they would be off. They were to go on Monday. The
Haddens came over on Saturday afternoon, just as Leslie
had nearly put the last things into her trunk, — a new
trunk, quite her own, with her initials in black paint upon
the russet leather at each end. On the bed lay her pretty
balmoral suit, made purposely for mountain wear, and just
finished. The young girls got together here, in Leslie's
chamber, of course.

"O how pretty! It's perfectly charming, — the love-
liest balmoral I ever saw in my life!" cried Jeannie
Hadden, seizing upon it instantly as she entered the room.
"Why, you'll look like a hamadryad, all in these wood-
browns!"

It was an uncommonly pretty striped petticoat, in two
alternating shades of dark and golden b own, with just a
hair-line of black defining their edges; and the border
was one broad, soft, velvety band of black, and a narrower
one following it above and below, easing the contrast and
blending the colors. The jacket, or rather shirt, finished
at the waist with a bit of a polka frill, was a soft flannel,
of the bright brown shade, braided with the darker hue,

and with black; and two pairs of bright brown raw-silk stockings, marked transversely with mere thread-lines of black, completed the mountain outfit.

"Yes; all I want is — " said Leslie, stopping short as she took up the hat that lay there also, — a last summer's hat, a plain black straw, with a slight brim, and ornamented only with a round lace veil and two bits of ostrich feather. "But never mind! It'll do well enough!"

As she laid it down again and ceased speaking, Cousin Delight came in, straight from Boston, where she had been doing two days' shopping; and in her hand she carried a parcel in white paper. I was going to say a round parcel, which it would have been but for something which ran out in a sharp tangent from one side, and pushed the wrappings into an odd angle. This she put into Leslie's hands.

"A fresh — fig-leaf — for you, my dear."

"What *does* she mean?" cried the Haddens, coming close to see.

"Only a little Paradise-fashion of speech between Cousin Del and me," said Leslie, coloring a little and laughing, while she began, somewhat hurriedly, to remove the wrappings.

"What have you done? And how did you come to think?" she exclaimed, as the thing enclosed appeared: a round brown straw turban, — not a staring turban, but one of those that slope with a little graceful downward droop upon the brow, — bound with a pheasant's breast, the wing shooting out jauntily, in the tangent I mentioned, over the right ear; — all in bright browns, in lovely harmony with the rest of the hamadryad costume.

"It's no use to begin to thank you, Cousin Del. It's just one of the things you're always doing, and rejoice in doing." The happy face was full of loving thanks, plainer than many words. "Only you're a kind of a *sarpent* yourself, after all, I'm afraid, with your beguilements. I wonder if you thought of that," whispered Leslie, merrily, while the others *oh-oh'd* over the gift. "What else do you think I shall be good for when I get all those on?"

"I'll venture you," said Cousin Delight; and the trifling words conveyed a real, earnest confidence, the best possible antidote to the "beguilement."

"One thing is funny," said Jeannie Hadden, suddenly, with an accent of demur. "We're all pheasants. *Our* new hats are pheasants, too. I don't know what Augusta will think of such a covey of us."

"O, it's no matter," said Elinor. "This is a golden pheasant, on brown straw, and ours are purple, on black. Besides, we all *look* different enough."

"I suppose it doesn't signify," returned Jeannie; "and if Augusta thinks it does, she may just give me that black and white plover of hers I wanted so. I think our complexions *are* all pretty well suited."

This was true. The fair hair and deep blue eyes of Elinor were as pretty under the purple plumage as Jeannie's darker locks and brilliant bloom; and there was a wonderful bright mingling of color between the golden pheasant's breast and the gleaming chestnut waves it crowned, as Leslie took her hat and tried it on.

This was one of the little touches of perfect taste and adaptation which could sometimes make Leslie Goldthwaite almost beautiful; and was there ever a girl of fifteen who would not like to be beautiful if she could? This wish, and the thought and effort it would induce, were likely to be her great temptation. Passably pretty girls, who may, with care, make themselves often more than passable, have far the hardest of it with their consciences about these things; and Leslie had a conscience, and was reflective for her age, — and we have seen how questions had begun to trouble her.

A Sunday between a packing and a journey is a trying day always. There are the trunks, and it is impossible not to think of the getting up and getting off to-morrow; and one hates so to take out fresh sleeves and collars and pocket-handkerchiefs, and to wear one's nice white skirts. It is a Sunday put off, too probably, with but odds and ends of thought, as well as apparel.

Leslie went to church, of course, — the Goldthwaites were always regular in this, — and she wore her quiet straw bonnet. Mrs. Goldthwaite had a feeling that hats were rather pert and coquettish for the sanctuary. Nevertheless they met the Haddens in the porch, in the glory of their purple pheasant plumes, whereof the long tail-feathers made great circles in the air as the young heads turned this way and that, in the excitement of a few snatched words before they entered.

The organ was playing; and the low, deep, tremulous rumble that an organ gives sometimes, when it seems to creep under and vibrate all things with a strange, vital thrill, overswept their trivial chat, and made Leslie almost shiver. " O, I wish they would n't do that," she said, turning to go in.

" What ? " said Jeannie Hadden, unaware.

" Touch the nerve.　The great nerve — of creation."

" What queer things Les' Goldthwaite says sometimes,"
whispered Elinor ; and they passed the inner door.

The Goldthwaites sat two pews behind the Haddens.
Leslie could not help thinking how elegant Mrs. Linceford was, as she swept in, in her rich black silk, and real
lace shawl, and delicate, costly bonnet ; and the perfectly

gloved hand that upheld a bit of extravagance in Valenciennes lace and cambric made devotion seem — what? The more graceful and touching in one who had all this world's luxuries, or — almost a mockery?

The pheasant-plumed hats went decorously down in prayer-time, but the tail-feathers ran up perker than ever, from the posture; Leslie saw this, because she had lifted her own head and unclosed her eyes in a self-indignant honesty, when she found on what her secret thoughts were running. Were other people so much better than she? And *could* they do both things? How much was right in all this that was outwardly so beguiling? and where did the "serving Mammon" begin.

Was everything so much intenser and more absorbing with her than with the Haddens? Why could she not take things as they came, as these girls did, or seemed to do? Be glad of her pretty things, — her pretty looks even, — her coming pleasures, — with no misgivings or self-searchings, and then turn round and say her prayers properly?

Wasn't beauty put into the world for the sake of beauty? And wasn't it right to love it, and make much of it, and multiply it? What were arts and human ingenuities for, and the things given to work with? All this grave weighing of a great moral question was in the mind of the young girl of fifteen again this Sunday morning. Such doubts and balancings begin far earlier, often, than we are apt to think.

The minister shook hands cordially and respectfully with Mrs. Linceford after church. He had no hesitation at her stylishness and fineries. Everybody took every·

body else for granted ; and it was all right, Leslie Goldthwaite supposed, except in her own foolish, unregulated
thoughts. Everybody else had done their Sunday duty,
and it was enough ; only she had been all wrong and
astray, and in confusion. There was a time for everything,
only her times and thoughts would mix themselves up
and interfere. Perhaps she was very weak-minded, and
the only way for her would be to give it all up, and wear
drab, or whatever else might be most unbecoming, and be
fiercely severe, mortifying the flesh. She got over that
— her young nature reacting — as they all walked up
the street together, while the sun shone down smilingly
upon the world in Sunday best, and the flowers were gay
in the door-yards, and Miss Milliken's shop was reveren-
tial with the green shutters before the windows that had
been gorgeous yesterday with bright ribbons and fresh
fashions ; and there was something thankful in her feeling of the pleasantness that was about her, and a certainty that she should only grow morose if she took to
resisting it all. She would be as good as she could, and
let the pleasantness and the prettiness come "by the
way." Yes, that was just what Cousin Delight had said.
"All these things shall be added," — was not that the
Gospel word ? So her troubling thought was laid for the
hour ; but it should come up again. It was in the
"seeking first" that the question lay. By and by she
would go back of the other to this, and see clearer, — in
the light, perhaps, of something that had been already
given her, and which, as she lived on toward a fuller
readiness for it, should be "brought to her remem-
brance."

Monday brought the perfection of a traveller's morn‑
ing.   There had been a shower during the night, and
the highways lay cool, moist, and dark-brown between
the green of the fields and the clean-washed, red-brick
pavements of the town.   There would be no dust even
on the railroad, and the air was an impalpable draught of
delight.   To the three young girls, standing there under
the station-portico, — for they chose the smell of the
morning rather than the odors of apples and cakes and
indescribables which go to make up the distinctive atmos‑
phere of a railway waiting-room, — there was but one
thing to be done to-day in the world ; — one thing for
which the sun rose, and wheeled himself toward that
point in the heavens which would make eight o'clock
down below.   Of all the ships that might sail this day
out of harbors, or the trains that might steam out of cities
across states, they recked nothing but of this that was to
take them toward the hills.   There were unfortunates,
doubtless, bound elsewhere, by peremptory necessity ;
there were people who were going nowhere, but about
their daily work and errands ; all these were simply to
be pitied, or wondered at, as to how they could feel *not*
to be going upon a mountain journey.   It is queer to
think, on a last Thursday in November, or on a Fourth
of July, of States where there may not be a Thanksgiv‑
ing, or of far-off lands that have no Independence day.
It was just as strange, somehow, to imagine how this
day, that was to them the culminating point of so much
happy anticipation, the beginning of so much certain joy,
could be otherwise, and yet be anything to the super‑
numerary people who filled up around them the life that

ιentred in just this to them. Yet in truth it was, to most folks, simply a fair Monday morning, and an excellent "drying day."

They bounded off along the iron track,—the great steam-pulse throbbed no faster than in time to their bright, young eagerness. It had been a momentous matter to decide upon their seats, of which there had been opportunity for choice when they entered the car ; at last they had been happily settled, face to face, by the good-natured removal of a couple of young farmers, who saw that the four ladies wished to be seated together. Their hand-bags were hung up, their rolls of shawls disposed beneath their feet, and Mrs. Linceford had taken out her novel. The Haddens had each a book also in her bag, to be perfectly according to rule in their equipment ; but they were not old travellers enough to care to begin upon them yet. As to Leslie Goldthwaite, *her* book lay ready open before her, for long, contented reading, in two chapters, both visible at once ;—the broad, open country, with its shifting pictures and suggestions of life and pleasantness ; and the carriage interior, with its dissimilar human freight, and its yet more varied hints of history and character and purpose.

She made a story in her own mind, half unconsciously, of every one about her. Of the pretty girl alone, with no elaborate travelling arrangements, going only, it was evident, from one way-station to another, perhaps to spend a summer day with a friend. Of the stout old country grandmamma, with a basket full of doughnuts and early apples, that made a spiciness and orchard fragrance all about her, and that she surely never meant to eat her-

2

self, seeing, first, that she had not a tooth in her head,
and also that she made repeated anxious requests of the
conductor, catching him by the coat-skirts as he passed,
to "let her know in season when they began to get into
Bartley"; who asked, confidentially, of her next neigh-
bor, a well-dressed elderly gentleman, if "he did n't
think it was about as cheap comin' by the cars as it
would ha' ben to hire a passage any other way?" and innocently endured the smile that her query called forth
on half a dozen faces about her.   The gentleman, *without*
a smile, courteously lowered his newspaper to reply that
"he always thought it better to avail one's self of established conveniences rather than to waste time in inde-
pendent contrivances"; and the old lady sat back, — as
far back as she dared, considering her momentary apprehension of Bartley, — quite happily complacent in the
confirmation of her own wisdom.

There was a trig, not to say prim, spinster, without a
vestige of comeliness in her face, save the comeliness of
a clear, clean, energetic expression, — such as a new
broom or a bright tea-kettle might have, suggesting capacity for house-thrift and hearth-comfort, — who wore a
gray straw bonnet, clean and neat as if it had not lasted
for six years at least, which its fashion evidenced, and
which, having a bright green tuft of artificial grass stuck
arbitrarily upon its brim by way of modern adornment,
put Leslie mischievously in mind of a roof so old that
blades had sprouted in the eaves.   She was glad afterwards that she had not spoken her mischief.

What made life beautiful to all these people?   These
farmers, who put on at daybreak their coarse homespun,

for long hours of rough labor? These homely, home-bred women, who knew nothing of graceful fashions, — who had always too much to do to think of elegance in doing? Perhaps that was just it; they had always something to do, something outside of themselves; in their honest, earnest lives there was little to tempt them to a frivolous self-engrossment. Leslie touched close upon the very help and solution she wanted, as she thought these thoughts.

Opposite to her there sat a poor man, to whom there had happened a great misfortune. One eye was lost, and the cheek was drawn and marked by some great scar of wound or burn. One half his face was a fearful blot. How did people bear such things as these, — to go

through the world knowing that it could never be pleasant to any human being to look upon them? that an instinct of pity and courtesy even would turn every casual
glance away? There was a strange, sorrowful pleading
in the one expressive side of the man's countenance,
and a singularly untoward incident presently called it
forth, and made it almost ludicrously pitiful. A bustling
fellow entered at a way-station, his arms full of a great
frame that he carried. As he blundered along the passage, looking for a seat, a jolt of the car, in starting,
pitched him suddenly into the vacant place beside this
man; and the open expanse of the large looking-glass —
for it was that which the frame held — was fairly smitten,
like an insult of fate, into the very face of the unfortunate.

"Beg pardon," the new-comer said, in an off-hand
way, as he settled himself, holding the glass full before
the other while he righted it; and then, for the first
time, giving a quick glance toward him. The astonishment — the intuitive repulsion — the consciousness of
what he had done, betokened by the instant look of the
one man, and the helpless, mute "How could you?" that
seemed spoken in the strange, uprolled, one-sided expression of the other, — these involuntarily-met regards made
a brief concurrence at once sad and irresistibly funny, as
so many things in this strange life are.

The man of the mirror inclined his burden quietly the
other way; and now it reflected the bright faces opposite, under the pheasant plumes. Was it any delight
to Leslie to see her own face so? What was the use of
being — what right had she to wish to be — pretty and
pleasant to look at, when there were such utter lifelong

loss and disfigurement in the world for others? Why should it not as well happen to her? And how did the world seem to such a person, and where was the *worthwhile* of it? This was the question which lingered last in her mind, and to which all else reverted. *To be able to bear;* perhaps this was it; and this was greater, indeed, than any outer grace.

Such as these were the wayside meanings that came to Leslie Goldthwaite that morning in the first few hours of her journey. Meanwhile, Jeannie and Elinor Hadden had begun to be tired; and Mrs. Linceford, not much entertained with her novel, held it half closed over her finger, drew her brown veil closely, and sat with her eyes shut, compensating herself with a doze for her early rising. Had the same things come to these? Not precisely; something else, perhaps. In all things, one is still taken and another left. I can only follow, minutely, one.

III.

THE road left the flat farming country now, and turned
northward, up the beautiful river valley. There was
plenty to enjoy outside; and it was growing more and
more lovely with almost every mile. They left the great
towns gradually behind; each succeeding one seemed more
simply rural. Young girls were gathered on the platforms
at the little stations where they stopped sometimes; it
was the grand excitement of the place, — the coming of
the train, — and to these village lasses was what the
piazzas or the springs are to gay dwellers at Saratoga.

By dinner time they steamed up to the stately back
staircase of the " Pemigewasset." In the little parlor
where they smoothed their hair and rested a moment
before going to the dining-hall, they met again the lady
of the grass-grown bonnet. She took this off, making
herself comfortable, in her primitive fashion, for dinner;
and then Leslie noticed how little it was from any poverty
of nature that the fair and abundant hair, at least, had not
been made use of to take down the severe primness of
her outward style. It did take it down, in spite of all,
the moment the gray straw was removed. The great
round coil behind was all real, and *solid*, though it was
wound about with no thought save of security, and fastened with a buffalo-horn comb. Hair was a matter of
course; the thing was, to keep it out of the way; that
was what the fashion of this head expressed, and nothing
more. Where it was tucked over the small ears, — and

native refinement or the other thing shows very plainly in the ears, — it lay full, and shaped into a soft curve. She was only plain, not ugly, after all; and they are very different things, — there being a beauty of plainness in men and women, as there is in a rich fabric, sometimes.

Elinor Hadden stood by a window with her back to the others, while Leslie was noticing these things. She did not complain at first; one does n't like to allow, at once, that the toothache, or a mischance like this that had happened to her, is an established fact, — one is in for it the moment one does that. But she had got a cinder in her eye; and though she had winked, and stared, and rolled her eyelid under, and tried all the approved and instinctive means, it seemed persistent; and she was forced at last, just as her party was going in to dinner, to acknowledge that this traveller's misery had befallen her, and to make up her mind to the pain and wretchedness and ugliness of it for hours, if not even for days. Her face was quite disfigured already; the afflicted eye was bloodshot, and the whole cheek was red with tears and rubbing; she could only follow blindly along, her handkerchief up, and, half groping into the seat offered her, begin comfortlessly to help herself to some soup with her left hand. There was leaning across to inquire and pity; there were half a dozen things suggested, to which she could only reply, forlornly and impatiently, " I 've tried it." None of them could eat much, or with any satisfaction; this atom in the wrong place set everything wrong all at once with four people who, till now, had been so cheery.

The spinster lady was seated at some little distance down, on the opposite side. She began to send quick,

interested glances over at them; to make little half-
starts toward them, as if she would speak; and at last,
leaving her own dinner unfinished, she suddenly pushed
back her chair, got up, and came round. She touched
Elinor Hadden on the shoulder, without the least ado
of ceremony. "Come out here with me," she said. "I
can set you right in half a minute"; — and, confident
of being followed, moved off briskly out of the long hall.

Elinor gave a one-sided, questioning glance at her sisters, before she complied, reminding Leslie comically of
the poor, one-eyed man in the cars; and presently, with
a little hesitation, Mrs. Linceford and Jeannie compro-
mised the matter by rising themselves and accompany-
ing Elinor from the room. Leslie, of course, went also.

The lady had her gray bonnet on when they got back
to the little parlor; there is no time to lose in mere waiting for anything at a railway dining-place; and she had
her bag — a veritable, old-fashioned, home-made carpet
thing — open on a chair before her, and in her hand a
long, knit purse with steel beads and rings. Out of this
she took a twisted bit of paper, and from the paper a
minute something which she popped between her lips as
she replaced the other things. Then she just beckoned,
hastily, to Elinor.

"It's only an eyestone; did you ever have one in?
Well, you need n't be afraid of it; I 've had 'em in
hundreds of times. You would n't know 't was there,
and it 'll just ease all the worry; and by and by it 'll
drop out of itself, cinder and all. They 're terribly teasing things, cinders; and somebody 's always sure to get
one. I always keep three eyestones in my purse. You

need n't mind my not having it back; I 've got a little
glass bottle full at home, and it 's wonderful the sight of
comfort they 've been to folks."

Elinor shrunk; Mrs. Linceford showed a little high-
bred demur about accepting the offered aid of their
unknown travelling-companion ; but the good woman
comprehended nothing of this, and went on insisting.

"You 'd better let me put it in right off; it 's only
just to drop it under the eyelid, and it 'll work round
till it finds the speck. But you can take it and put it
in yourself, when you 've made up your mind, if you 'd
rather." With which she darted her head quickly from
side to side, looking about the room, and, spying a scrap
of paper on a table, had the eyestone twisted in it in an
instant, and pressed it into Elinor's hand. "You 'll be
glad enough of it, yet," said she, and then took up her
bag, and moved quickly off among the other passengers
descending to the train.

"What a funny woman, to be always carrying eyestones about, and putting them in people's eyes ! " said
Jeannie.

"It was quite kind of her, I 'm sure," said Mrs. Linceford, with a mingling in her tone of acknowledgment and
of polite tolerance for a great liberty. When elegant
people break their necks or their limbs, common ones
may approach and assist; as, when a house takes fire,
persons get in who never did before ; and perhaps a
suffering eye may come into the catalogue of misfor-
tunes sufficient to equalize differences for the time being.
But it *is* queer for a woman to make free to go without
her own dinner to offer help to a stranger in pain.   Not

2*   c

many people, in any sense of the word, go about provided with eyestones against the chance cinders that may
worry others.   Something in this touched Leslie Goldthwaite with a curious sense of a beauty in living that
was not external.

If it had not been for Elinor's mishap and inability to
enjoy, it would have been pure delight from the very
beginning, this afternoon's ride.   They had their seats
upon the "mountain side," where the view of the
thronging hills was like an ever-moving panorama ; as,
winding their way farther and farther up into the heart
of the wild and beautiful region, the horizon seemed
continually to fill with always vaster shapes, that lifted
themselves, or emerged, over and from behind each
other, like mustering clans of giants, bestirred and curious, because of the invasion among their fastnesses of
this sprite of steam.

"Where you can come down, I can go up," it seemed to
fizz, in its strong, exulting whisper, to the river ; passing
it always, yet never getting by ; tracking, step by step,
the great stream backward toward its small beginnings.

"See, there are real blue peaks!" cried Leslie, joyously, pointing away to the north and east, where the
outlines lay faint and lovely in the far distance.

"O, I wish I could see! I'm losing it all!" said Elinor,
plaintively and blindfold.

"Why don't you try the eyestone?" said Jeannie.

But Elinor shrunk, even yet, from deliberately putting
that great thing in her eye, agonized already by the presence of a mote.

There came a touch on her shoulder, as before.   The

good woman of the gray bonnet had come forward from her seat farther down the car.

"I'm going to stop presently," she said, at "East Haverhill; and I *should* feel more satisfied in my mind if you'd just let me see you easy before I go. Besides, if you don't do something quick, the cinder will get so bedded in, and make such an inflammation, that a dozen eyestones would n't draw it out."

At this terror, poor Elinor yielded, in a negative sort of way. She ceased to make resistance when her unknown friend, taking the little twist of paper from the hand still fast closed over it with the half-conscious grasp of pain, dexterously unrolled it, and produced the wonderful chalky morsel.

"Now, 'let's see, says the blind man'"; and she drew down hand and handkerchief with determined yet gentle touch. "Wet it in your own mouth"; — and the eyestone was between Elinor's lips before she could refuse or be aware. Then one thumb and finger was held to take it again, while the other made a sudden pinch at the lower eyelid, and, drawing it at the outer corner before it could so much as quiver away again, the little white stone was slid safely under.

"Now 'wink as much as you please,' as the man said that took an awful looking daguerreotype of me once. Good by. Here's where I get out. And there they all are to meet me." And then, the cars stopping, she made her way, with her carpet-bag and parasol and a great newspaper bundle, gathered up hurriedly from goodness knows where, along the passage, and out upon the platform.

" Why, it 's the strangest thing ! I don't feel it in the least ! Do you suppose it ever *will* come out again, Augusta ? " cried Elinor, in a tone greatly altered from any in which she had spoken for two hours.

" Of course it will," cried " Gray-bonnet " from beneath the window. " Don't be under the least mite oi concern about anything but looking out for it when *i* does, to keep it against next time."

Leslie saw the plain, kindly woman surrounded in a minute by half a dozen young eager welcomers and claimants, and a whole history came out in the unreserved exclamations of the few instants for which the train delayed.

" O, it 's *such* a blessing you 've come ! I don't know as Emma Jane would have been married at all if you had n't ! "

" We warn't sure you 'd get the letter."

" Or as Aunt 'Nisby would spare you."

" 'Life wanted to come over on his crutches. He 's just got his new ones, and he gets about first rate. But we would n't let him beat himself out for to-morrow."

" How *is* 'Life ? "

" Hearty as would any way be consistent — with oneleggedness. He 'd never 'a got back, we all know, if you had n't gone after him." It was a young man's voice that spoke these last sentences, and it grew tender at the end.

" You 're to trim the cake," began one of the young girls again, crowding up. " She says nobody else can. Nobody else *ever* can. And " — with a little more mystery — " there 's the veil to fix. She says you 're used

to wedd'n's, and know about veils; and you was down to Lawrence at Lorany's. And she wants things in *real style*. She's dreadful *pudjicky*, Emma Jane is; she won't have anything without it's exactly right."

The plain face was full of beaming sympathy and readiness; the stiff-looking spinster-woman, with the " grass in the eaves of her bonnet," — grass grown also over many an old hope in her own life, may be, — was here in the midst of young joy and busy interest, making them all her own ; had come on purpose, looked for and hailed as the one without whom nothing could ever be done, — more tenderly yet, as one but for whom some brave life and brother love would have gone down. In the midst of it all she had had ear and answer, to the very last, for the stranger she had comforted on her way. What difference did it make whether she wore an old bonnet with green grass in it, or a round hat with a gay feather? — whether she were fifteen or forty-five, but for the good she had had time to do? — whether Lorany's wedding down at Lawrence had been really a stylish fes- tival or no? There was a beauty here which verily shone out through all ; and such a life should have no time to be tempted.

The engine panted, and the train sped on. She never met her fellow-traveller again, but these things Leslie Goldthwaite had learned from her, — these things she laid by silently in her heart. And the woman in the gray bonnet never knew the half that she had done.

After taking one through wildernesses of beauty, after whirling one past nooks where one could gladly linger whole summers, it is strange at what commonplace and

graceless termini these railroads contrive to land one.
Lovely Wells River, where the road makes its sharp
angle, and runs back again until it strikes out eastward
through the valley of the Ammonoosuc, — where the
waters leap to each other, and the hills bend round in
majestic greeting, — where our young party cried out, in
an ignorance at once blessed and pathetic, " O, if Littleton should only be like this, or if we could stop here ! "
— yet where one cannot stop, because here there is no
regular stage connection, and nothing else to be found,
very probably, that travellers might want, save the out-
door glory, — Wells River and Woodville were left behind, lying in the evening stillness of June, — in the
grand and beautiful disregard of things greater than the
world is rushing by to seek, — and for an hour more
they threaded through fair valley sweeps and reaches,
past solitary hillside clearings, and detached farms, and
the most primitive of mountain hamlets, where the limit
and sparseness of neighborhood drew forth from a gentleman sitting behind them — come, doubtless, from some
suburban home, where numberless household wants kept
horse and wagon perpetually on the way for city or village — the suggestive query, " I wonder what they do
here when they're out of saleratus ? " This brought
them up, as against a dead wall of dreariness and disappointment, at the Littleton station.   It had been managed
as it always is ; the train had turned most ingeniously
into a corner whence there was scarcely an outlook upon
anything of all the magnificence that must yet be lying
close about them ; and here was only a tolerably well-
populated country town, filled up to just the point that

excludes the picturesque and does not attain to the
highly civilized. And into the heart of this they were to
be borne, and to be shut up there this summer night,
with the full moon flooding mountain and river, and the
woods whispering up their peace to heaven.

It was bad enough, but worse came. The hotel coach
was waiting, and they hastened to secure their seats, giving their checks to the driver, who disappeared with a
handful of these and others, leaving his horses with the
reins tied to the dash-board, and a boy ten years old
upon the box.

There were heads out anxiously at either side, between concern for safety of body and of property. Mrs.
Linceford looked uneasily toward the confused group
upon the platform, from among whom luggage began to
be drawn out in a fashion regardless of covers and
corners. The large russet trunk with the black H, —
the two linen-cased ones with " Hadden " in full, — the
two square bonnet-boxes, — these, one by one, were
dragged and whirled toward the vehicle and jerked upon
the rack ; but the " ark," as they called Mrs. Linceford's huge light French box, and the one precious re-
ceptacle that held all Leslie's pretty outfit, where were
these?

" Those are not all, driver ! There is a high black
French trunk, and a russet leather one."

" Got all you give me checks for, — seb'm pieces " ;
and he pointed to two strange articles of luggage waiting
their turn to be lifted up, — a long, old-fashioned gray
hair trunk, with letters in brass nails upon the lid, and
as antiquated a carpet-bag, strapped and padlocked across

the mouth, suggestive in size and fashion of the United States mail.

"Never saw them before in my life! There's some dreadful mistake! What *can* have become of ours?"

"Can't say, ma'am, I'm sure. Don't often happen. But them was your checks."

Mrs. Linceford leaned back for an instant in a breathless despair. "I must get out and see."

"If you please, ma'am. But 't ain't no use. The things is all cleared off." Then, stooping to examine the trunk, and turning over the bag, "Queer, too. These things is chalked all right for Littleton. Must ha' been a mistake with the checks, and somebody changed their minds on the way, — Plymouth, most likely, — and stopped with the wrong baggage. Wouldn't worry, ma'am; it's as bad for one as for t'other, any how, and they'll be along to-morrow, no kind o' doubt. Strays allers turns up on this here road. No danger about that. I'll see to havin' these 'ere stowed away in the baggage-room." And shouldering the bag, he seized the trunk by the handle and hauled it along over the rough embankment and up the steps, flaying one side as he went.

"But, dear me! what am I to do?" said Mrs. Linceford, piteously. "Everything in it that I want to-night, — my dressing-box and my wrappers and my air-cushion; they'll be sure not to have any bolsters on the beds, and only one feather in each corner of the pillows!"

But this was only the first surprise of annoyance. She recollected herself on the instant, and leaned back again, saying nothing more. She had no idea of amusing her

unknown stage-companions at any length with her fine-
lady miseries.   Only, just before they reached the hotel,
she added low to Jeannie, out of the unbroken train of
her own private lamentation, " And my rose-glycerine!
After all this dust and heat!   I feel parched to a mummy, and I shall be an object to behold ! "

Leslie sat upon her right hand.   She leaned closer,
and said quickly, glad of the little power to comfort, " I
have some rose-glycerine here in my bag."

Mrs. Linceford looked round at her; her face was
really bright.   As if she had not lost her one trunk
also !   " You are a phœnix of a travelling-companion,
you young thing !" the lady thought, and felt suddenly
ashamed of her own unwonted discomfiture.

Half an hour afterward Leslie Goldthwaite flitted across
the passage between the two rooms they had secured for
their party, with a bottle in her hand and a pair of pillows
over her arm.   " Ours is a double-bedded room, too, Mrs.
Linceford, and neither Elinor nor I care for more than one
pillow.   And here is the rose-glycerine."

These essential comforts, and the instinct of good-breed-
ing, brought the grace and the smile back fully to Mrs.
Linceford's face.   More than that, she felt a gratefulness,
and the contagion and emulation of cheerful patience under
a common misfortune.   She bent over and kissed Leslie
as she took the bottle from her hand.   " You 're a dear
little sunbeam," she said.   " We 'll send an imperative
message down the line, and have all our own traps again
to-morrow."

The collar that Elinor Hadden had lent Leslie was not
very becoming, the sleeves had enormous wristbands, and

were made for double sleeve-buttons, while her own were single ; moreover, the brown silk net, which she had supposed thoroughly trustworthy, had given way all at once into a great hole under the waterfall, and the soft hair would fret itself through and threaten to stray untidily. She had two such pretty nets in reserve in her missing trunk, and she did hate so to be in any way coming to pieces ! Yet there was somehow a feeling that repaid it all, and even quieted the real anxiety as to the final " turning up " of their fugitive property, — not a mere self-complacence, hardly a self-complacence at all, but a half-surprised gladness, that had something thankful in it. If she might not be all leaves, perhaps, after all ! If she really could, even in some slight thing, care most for the life and spirit underneath, to keep this sweet and pleasant, and the fruit of it a daily good, and not a bitterness, — if she could begin, by holding herself undisturbed, though obliged to wear a collar that stood up behind and turned over in front with those lappet corners she had always thought so ugly, — yes, even though the waterfall should leak out and ripple over stubbornly, — though these things must go on for twenty-four hours at least, and these twenty-four hours be spent unwillingly in a dull country tavern, where the windows looked out from one side into a village street, and from the other into stable and clothes yards ! There would be something for her to do, — to keep bright and help to keep the others bright. There was a hope in it; the life was more than raiment; it was better worth while than to have only got on the nice round collar and dainty cuffs that fitted and suited her, or even the little bead net that came over in a Marie Stuart point so prettily between the small crimped puffs of her hair.

A little matter, nothing to be self-applauding about, — only a straw; but — if it showed the possible way of the wind, the motive power that might be courted to set through her life, taking her out of the trade-currents of vanity? Might she have it in her, after all? Might she even be able to come, if need be, to the strength of mind for wearing an old gray straw bonnet, and bearing to be forty years old, and helping to adorn the young and beautiful for looks that never — just so — should be bent again on her?

Leslie Goldthwaite had read of martyr and hero sufferance all her life, as she had looked upon her poor, one-eyed fellow-traveller to-day; the pang of sympathy had always 'been, — " These things have been borne, are being borne, in the world; how much of the least of them could I endure, — I, looking for even the little things of life to be made smooth?" It depended, she began faintly and afar off to see, upon where the true life lay, — how far behind the mere outer covering vitality withdrew itself.

IV.

U P - - up — up, — from glory to glory!
This was what it seemed to Leslie Goldthwaite,
riding, that golden June morning, over the road that
threaded along, always climbing, the chain of hills that
could be climbed, into the nearer and nearer presence ot
those mountain majesties, penetrating farther and farther
into the grand solitudes sentinelled forever by their in-
accessible pride.

Mrs. Linceford had grown impatient; she had declared
it impossible, when the splendid sunshine of that next day
challenged them forth out of their dull sojourn, to remain
there twenty-four hours longer, waiting for anything.
Trunks or none, she would go on, and wait at Jefferson,
at least, where there was something to console one. All
possible precaution was taken; all possible promises were
made; the luggage should be sent on next day, — perhaps that very night; wagons were going and returning
often now; there would be no further trouble, they
might rest assured. The hotel-keeper had a "capital
team," — his very best, — at their instant service, if
they chose to go on this morning; it could be at the
door in twenty minutes. So it was chartered, and ordered round, — an open mountain wagon, with four
horses; their remaining luggage was secured upon it,
and they themselves took their seats, gayly.

"Who cares for trunks or boxes now?" Leslie cried
out in joyousness, catching the first, preparatory glimpse

of grandeur, when their road, that wound for a time through the low, wet valley-lands, began to ascend a rugged hillside, whence opened vistas that hinted something of the glory that was to come. All the morning long, these wheeled about them, and smiled out in the sunshine, or changed to grave, grand reticence under the cloud-shadows, those shapes of might and beauty that filled up earth and heaven.

Leslie grew silent, with the hours of over-full delight. Thoughts thronged in upon her. All that had been deepest and strongest in the little of life that she had lived wakened and lifted again in such transcendent presence. Only the high places of spirit can answer to these high places of God in his creation. .

Now and then, Jeannie and Elinor fell into their chatter, about their summer plans, and pleasures, and dress; about New York, and the new house Mrs. Linceford had taken in West Twenty-ninth Street, where they were to visit her next winter, and participate for the first time, under her matronizing, in city gayeties. Leslie wondered how they could; she only answered when appealed to; she felt as if people were jogging her elbow, and whispering distractions, in the midst of some noble eloquence.

The woods had a word for her; a question, and their own sweet answer of help. The fair June leafage was out in its young glory of vivid green; it reminded her of her talk with Cousin Delight.

" We *do* love leaves for their own sake; trees, and vines, and the very green grass, even." So she said to herself, asking still for the perfect parable that should solve and teach all.

It came, with the breath of wild grape-vines, hidden
somewhere in the wayside thickets. "Under the leaf
lies our tiny green blossom," it said; "and its perfume
is out on the air. Folded in the grass-blade is a feathery
bloom, of seed or grain; and by and by the fields will be
all waving with it. Be sure that the blossom is under the
leaf."

Elinor Hadden's sweet child-face, always gentle and
good-humored, though visited little yet with the deep
touch of earnest thought, — smiling upon life as life
smiled upon her, — looked lovelier to Leslie as this
whisper made itself heard in her heart; and it was with
a sweeter patience and a more believing kindliness that
she answered, and tried to enter into, her next merry
words.

There was something different about Jeannie. She
was older; there was a kind of hard determination sometimes with her, in turning from suggestions of graver
things; the child-unconsciousness was no longer there;
something restless, now and then defiant, had taken its
place; she had caught a sound of the deeper voices, but
her soul would not yet turn to listen. She felt the blossom of life yearning under the leaf; but she bent the
green beauty heedfully above it, and made believe it
was not there.

Looking into herself and about her with asking eyes,
Leslie had learned something already by which she ap-
prehended these things of others. Heretofore, her two
friends had seemed to her alike, — able, both of them, to
take life innocently and carelessly as it came; she began
now to feel a difference.

Her eyes were bent away off toward the Franconia hills, when Mrs. Linceford leaned round to look in them, and spoke, in the tone her voice had begun to take toward her. She felt one of her strong likings — her immense fancies, as she called them, which were really warm sympathies of the best of her with the best she found in the world — for Leslie Goldthwaite.

"It seems to me you are a *stray* sunbeam this morning," she said, in her winning way. "What kind of thoughts are going out so far? What is it all about?"

A verse of •the Psalms was ringing itself in Leslie's mind; had been there, under all the other vague musings and chance suggestions for many minutes of her silence. But she would not have spoken it — she *could* not — for all the world. She gave the lady one of the chance suggestions instead. "I have been looking down into that lovely hollow; it seems like a children's party, with all the grave grown folks looking on."

"Childhood and grown-up-hood; not a bad simile."

It was not indeed. It was a wild basin, within a group of the lesser hills close by; full of little feathery birches, that twinkled and played in the light breeze and gorgeous sunshine slanting in upon them between the slopes that lay in shadow above, — slopes clothed with ranks of dark pines and cedars and hemlocks, looking down seriously, yet with a sort of protecting tenderness, upon the shimmer and frolic they seemed to have climbed up out of. Those which stood in the half-way shadow were gravest. Hoar old stems upon the very tops were touched with the selfsame glory that lavished itself below. This also was no less a true similitude.

" Know ye not this parable?" the Master said. "How then shall ye know all parables?" Verily, they lie about us by the wayside, and the whole earth is vocal with the wisdom of the Lord.

I cannot go with our party step by step; I have a summer to spend with them. They came to Jefferson at noon, and sat themselves down in the solemn high court and council of the mountain kings. First, they must have rooms. In the very face of majesty they must settle their traps.

" You are lucky in coming in for one vacancy, made to-day," the proprietor said, throwing open a door that showed them a commodious second-floor corner-room, looking each way with broad windows upon the circle of glory, from Adams to Lafayette. A wide balcony ran along the southern side against the window which gave that aspect. There were two beds here, and two at least of the party must be content to occupy. Mrs. Linceford, of course; and it was settled that Jeannie should share it with her.

Up stairs, again, was choice of two rooms, — one flight or two. But the first looked out westward, where was comparatively little of what they had come for. Higher up, they could have the same outlook that the others had; a slanting ceiling opened with dormer window full upon the grandeur of Washington, and a second faced south-ward to where beautiful blue, dreamy Lafayette lay soft against the tender heaven.

" O, let us have this!" said Leslie, eagerly. "We don't mind stairs." And so it was settled.

" Only two days here?" they began to say, when they

gathered in Mrs. Linceford's room at nearly tea-time, after a rest and a freshening of their toilets.

" We might stay longer," Mrs. Linceford answered. " But the rooms are taken for us at Outledge, and one can't settle and unpack, when it's only a lingering from day to day. All there is here one sees from the windows. A great deal, to be sure; but it's all there at the first glance. We'll see how we feel on Friday."

" The Thoresbys are here, Augusta. I saw Ginevra on the balcony just now. They seem to have a large party with them. And I'm sure I heard them talk of a hop tonight. If your trunks would only come ! "

" They could not in time. They can only come in the train that reaches Littleton at six."

" But you'll go in, won't you? 'T is n't likely they dress much here, — though Ginevra Thoresby always dresses. Elinor and I could just put on our blue grenadines, and you've got plenty of things in your other boxes. One of your shawls is all you want, and we can lend Leslie something."

" I've only my thick travelling-boots," said Leslie; " and I should n't feel fit without a thorough dressing. It won't matter the first night, will it ? "

" Leslie Goldthwaite, you're getting slow ! Augusta ! "

" As true as I live, there is old Marmaduke Wharne ! "

" Let Augusta alone for not noticing a question till she chooses to answer it," said Jeannie Hadden, laughing. " And who, pray, is Marmaduke Wharne? With a name like that, if you did n't say ' old,' I should make up my mind to a real hero, right out of a book."

" He's an original. And — yes — he is a hero, — *out*

of a book, too, in his way. I met him at Catskill last
summer. He stayed there the whole season, till they
shut the house up and drove him down the mountain.
Other people came and went, took a look, and ran away;
but he was a fixture. He says he always does so, —
goes off somewhere and 'finds an Ararat,' and there
drifts up and sticks fast. In the winter he's in New
York; but that's a needle in a haystack. I never heard
of him till I found him at Catskill. He's an English-
man, and they say had more to his name once. It was
Wharne-*cliffe*, or Wharne-*leigh*, or something, and there's
a baronetcy in the family. I don't doubt, myself, that it's
his, and that a part of his oddity has been to drop it. He
was a poor preacher, years ago; and then, of a sudden,
he went out to England, and came back with plenty ot
money, and since then he's been an apostle and mission-
ary among the poor. That's his winter work; the summers, as I said, he spends in the hills. Most people are
half afraid of him; for he's one you'll get the blunt
truth from, if you never got it before. But come,
there's the gong, — ugh! how they batter it! — and
we must get through tea, and out upon the balcony, to
see the sunset and the 'purple light.' There's no time
now, girls, for blue grenadines; and it's always vulgar
to come out in a hurry with dress in a strange place."
And Mrs. Linceford gave a last touch to her hair,
straightened the things on her dressing-table, shut down
the lid of a box, and led the way from the room.

Out upon the balcony they watched the long, golden
going-down of the sun, and the creeping shadows, and
the purple half-light, and the after-smile upon the crests.

And then the heaven gathered itself in its night stillness, and the mountains were grand in the soft gloom, until the full moon came up over Washington.

There had been a few words of recognition with the Thoresby party, and then our little group had betaken itself to the eastern end of the piazza. After a while, one by one, the others strayed away, and they were left almost alone. There was a gathering and a sound of voices about the drawing-room, and presently came tho tones of the piano, struck merrily. They jarred, some-how, too; for the ringing, thrilling notes of a horn, blown below, had just gone down the diminishing echoes from cliff to cliff, and died into a listening silence, away over, one could not tell where beyond the mysterious ramparts.

"It's getting cold," said Jeannie, impatiently. "I think we've stayed here long enough. Augusta, *don't* you mean to get a proper shawl, and put some sort of lace thing on your head, and come in with us for a look, at least, at the hop? Come, Nell; come, Leslie; you might as well be at home as in a place like this, if you're only going to mope."

"It seems to me," said Leslie, more to herself than to Jeannie, looking over upon the curves and ridges and ravines of Mount Washington, showing vast and solemn under the climbing moon, "as if we had got into a cathe-dral!"

"And the 'great nerve' was being touched! Well, —that don't make *me* shiver. Besides, I didn't come here to shiver. I've come to have a right good time; and to look at the mountains — as much as is reasonable."

It was a pretty good definition of what Jeannie Hadden thought she had come into the world for. There was subtle indication in it, also, that the shadow of some doubt had not failed to touch her either, and that this with her was less a careless instinct than a resolved conclusion.

Elinor, in her happy good-humor, was ready for either thing; to stay in the night-splendor longer, or to go in. It ended in their going in. Outside, the moon wheeled on in her long southerly circuit, the stars trembled in their infinite depths, and the mountains abided in awful might. Within was a piano-tinkle of gay music, and demi-toilette, and demi-festival, — the poor, abridged reproduction of city revelry in the inadequate parlor of an unpretending mountain-house, on a three-ply carpet.

Marmaduke Wharne came and looked in at the doorway. Mrs. Linceford rose from her seat upon the sofa close by, and gave him courteous greeting. "The season has begun early, and you seem likely to have a pleasant summer here," she said, with the half-considered meaning of a common fashion of speech.

"No, madam!" answered Marmaduke Wharne, out of his real thought, with a blunt emphasis.

"You think not?" said Mrs. Linceford, suavely, in a quiet amusement. "It looks rather like it to-night."

"*This?* — It's no use for people to bring their bodies to the mountains, if they can't bring souls in them!" And Marmaduke Wharne turned on his heel, and, without further courtesy, strode away.

"What an old Grimgriffinhoof!" cried Jeannie,

under her breath; and Elinor laughed her little musical laugh of fun.

Mrs. Linceford drew up her shawl, and sat down again, the remnant of a well-bred smile upon her face. Leslie Goldthwaite rather wished old Marmaduke Wharne would come back again and say more. But this first glimpse of him was all they got to-night.

"Blown crystal clear by Freedom's northern wind."

Leslie said the last line of Whittier's glorious mountain sonnet, low, to herself, standing on the balcony
again that next morning, in the cold, clear breeze ; the
magnificent lines of the great earth-masses rearing themselves before her sharply against a cloudless morning sky,
defining and revealing themselves anew.

"Freedom's northern wind will take all the wave out ,
of your hair, and give you a red nose!" said Jeannie,
coming round from her room, and upon Leslie unaware.

Well, Jeannie *was* a pretty thing to look at, in her delicate blue cambric morning dress, gracefully braided with
white, with the fresh rose of recent sleep in her young
cheeks, and the gladness of young life in her dark eyes.
One might look away from the mountains to look at her ;
for, after all, the human beauty is the highest. Only, it
must express high things, or at last one turns aside.

"And there comes Marmaduke ; he 's worse than the
north wind. I can't stay to be 'blown clear' by him."
And Jeannie, in high, merry good-humor, flitted off.
It is easy to be merry and good-humored when one's
new dress fits exquisitely, and one's hair has n't been
fractious in the doing up.

Leslie had never, apparently to herself, cared less,
somehow, for self and little vanities ; it seemed as if it
were going to be quite easy for her, now and henceforth,
to care most for the nobler things of life. The great
mountain-enthusiasm had seized her for the first time,
and swept away before it all meaner thought ; and, besides, her trunk had been left behind, and she had nothing to put herself into but her plain brown travelling-
dress.

She let the wind play with the puffs of her hair, and
send some little light locks astray about her forehead.
She wrapped her shawl around her, and went and sat
where she had sat the night before, at the eastern end of
the balcony, her face toward the morning hills, as it had
been toward the evening radiance and purple shade.
Marmaduke Wharne was moving up and down, stopping
a little short of her when he turned, keeping his own soli-
tude as she kept hers. Faces and figures glanced out at
the hall-door for an instant each, and the keen salute of
the north-wind sent them invariably in again. Nobody
wanted to go with a red nose or tossed hair to the breakfast-table ; and breakfast was almost ready. But presently Mrs. Linceford came, and, seeing Mr. Wharne,
who always interested and amused her, she ventured
forth, bidding him good morning.

"Good morning, madam. It *is* a good morning."

"A little sharp, is n't it?" she said, shrugging her
shoulders together, irresolute about further lingering.
"Ah, Leslie? Let me introduce you to the Reverend
Mr. Wharne. My young friend and travelling companion, Miss Leslie Goldthwaite, Mr. Wharne. Have you
two driven everybody else off, or is it the nipping air?"

"I think it is either that they have not said their prayers this morning, or that they don't know their daily
bread when they see it. They think it is only saleratus
cakes and maple molasses.".

"As cross this morning as last night?" the lady ques-
tioned playfully.

"Not cross at all, Mrs. Linceford. Only jarred upon
continually by these people we have here just now. It

was different two years ago. But Jefferson is getting to
be too well known. The mountain places are being
spoiled, one after another."

"People will come. You can't help that."

"Yes, they will come, and frivel about the gates, without ever once entering in. 'Who shall ascend into the
hill of the Lord? And who shall stand in his holy
place? He that hath clean hands and a pure heart;
who hath not lifted up his soul unto vanity.'"

Leslie Goldthwaite's face quickened and glowed; they
were the psalm-lines that had haunted her thought yesterday, among the opening visions of the hill-country.
Marmaduke Wharne bent his keen eyes upon her, from
under their gray brows, noting her narrowly. She wist
not that she was noted, or that her face shone.

"One soul here, at least!" was what the stern old
man said to himself in that moment.

He was cynical and intolerant here among the mountains, where he felt the holy places desecrated, and the
gift of God unheeded. In the haunts of city misery
and vice, — misery and vice shut in upon itself, with no
broad outlook to the heavens, — he was tender, with
the love of Christ himself.

"'My house shall be called the house of prayer; but
these have made it a den of thieves.' It is true not alone
of the temples built with hands."

"Is that fair? How do you *know*, Mr. Wharne?"
The sudden, impetuous questions come from Leslie Goldthwaite.

"I see — what I see."

"The whole?" said Leslie, more restrainedly. She

remembered her respect for age and office. Yet she felt
sorely tempted, shy, proud girl as she was, to take up
cudgels for her friends, at least. Mr. Wharne liked her
the better for that.

" They turn away from this, with five words, — the
toll of custom, — or half a look, when the wind is north ;
and they go in to what you saw last night."

" After all, is n't it just *enjoyment*, either way ? May
n't one be as selfish as the other ? People were kind,
and bright, and pleasant with each other last night. Is
that a bad thing ? "

" No, little girl, it is not." And Marmaduke Wharne
came nearer to Leslie, and looked at her with a gentle
look that was wonderfully beautiful upon his stern gray
face. " Only, I would have a kindness that should go
deep, — coming from a depth. There are two things for
live men and women to do. To receive, from God ; and
to give out, to their fellows. One cannot be done without the other. No fruit, without the drinking of the
sunshine. No true tasting of the sunshine that is not
gathering itself toward the ripening of fruit."

Here it was again ; more teaching to the selfsame
point, — as we always do get it, with a seeming strange-
ness, whether it be for mind only, or for soul. You never
heard of a new name, or fact in history, that did not come
out again presently in some fresh or further mention or
allusion. It is the tender training of Him before whom
our life is of so great value.

At this moment, the gong sounded again ; saleratus
cakes and maple molasses were ready ; and they all
went in.

3 *

Leslie saw Imogen Thoresby change seats with her
mother, because the draft from the door was less in her
place; and take the pale top-cake from the plate, leaving
a brown one for the mother. Everybody likes brown
cakes best; and it was very unbecoming to sit opposite a
great, unshaded window, to say nothing of the draft.
Surely a little blossom peeped out here from under the
leaf. Leslie thought Imogen Thoresby might be forgiven
for having done her curls so elaborately, and put on such
an elegant wrapper; even for having ventured only a
half-look out at the balcony door, when she found the
wind was north. The parable was already teaching her
both ways.

I do not mean to preach upon every page. I have
begun by trying to tell you how a great influencing
thought was given into Leslie Goldthwaite's life, and
began to unravel for her perplexing questions that had
troubled her, — questions that come, I think, to many a
young girl just entering upon the world, as they came to
her; — how, in the simple history of her summer among
the mountains, a great deal solved itself and grew clear.
I would like to succeed in making you divine this, as you
follow out the simple history itself.

"Just in time!" cried Jeannie Hadden, running up
into Leslie's room at mid-afternoon that day. "There's
a stage over from Littleton, and your trunk is being
brought up this minute."

"And the hair-trunk and the mail-bag came on, too,
after all, and the queerest people with them!" added
Elinor, entering behind her.

They both stood back and were silent, as a man came

heavily along the passage with the trunk upon his shoulder.
He set it down and unfastened the straps, and in a minute
more was gone, and Leslie had the lid open. All there,
just as it had been in her own room at home three days
ago. Her face brightened, seeing her little treasures again.
She had borne it well; she had been able to enjoy without them; but she was very glad that they were come.

"It's nice that dinner is at lunch-time here, and that
nobody dresses until now. Make haste, and get on something pretty. Augusta won't let us get out organdies,
but we're determined on the blue grenadines. It's
awfully hot, — hot enough for anything. Do your hair
over the high rats, just for once."

"I always get into such a fuss with them, and I can't
bear to waste the time. How will this do?" Leslie
unpinned from its cambric cover a gray iron barège,
with a narrow puffing round the hem of the full skirt
and the little pointed bertha cape. With it lay bright
cherry ribbons for the neck and hair.

"Lovely! Make haste and come down to our room." .
And having to dress herself, Jeannie ran off again, and
Elinor shut the door.

It was nice to have on everything fresh; to have got
her feet into rosetted slippers instead of heavy balmoral
boots; to feel the lightness and grace of her own movement as she went down stairs and along the halls in
floating folds of delicate barège, after wearing the close,
uncomfortable travelling-dress, with the sense of dust
and fatigue that clung about it; to have a little flutter
of bright ribbon in her hair, that she knew was, as
Elinor said "the prettiest part of ner." It was pleas-

ant to see Mrs. Linceford look pleased, as she opened her door to her, and to have her say, "You always do get on exactly the right thing!" There was a fresh feeling of pleasure even in looking over at Washington, sun-lighted and shadowed in his miles of heights and depths, as she sat by the cool east window, feeling quite her dainty self again. Dress is but the outside thing, as beauty is but "skin deep"; but there is a deal of inevitable skin-sensation, pleasurable or uncomfortable, and Leslie had a good right to be thoroughly comfortable now.

The blinds to the balcony window were closed; that led to a funny little episode presently, — an odd commentary on the soul-and-body question, as it had come up to them in graver fashion.

Outside, to two chairs just under the window, came a couple newly arrived, — the identical proprietors of the exchanged luggage. It was an elderly countryman, and his home-bred, matter-of-fact wife. They too had had their privations and anxieties, and the outset of their evidently unusual travels had been marred in its pleasure. In plain truth, the good woman was manifestly soured by her experience.

Right square before the blinds she turned her back, unconscious of the audience within, lifted her elbows, like clothes-poles, to raise her draperies, and settled herself with a dissatisfied flounce, that expressed beforehand what she was about to put in words. "For *my* part," she announced, deliberately, "I think the White Mountains is a clear — *hummux!*"

"Good large hummocks, any way," returned her companion.

" You know what I mean. 'T ain't worth comin' for.
Losin' baggage, an' everything. We'd enough sight
better ha' stayed at Plymouth. An' if it had n't a ben for
your dunderheadedness, givin' up the checks an' never
stoppin' to see what was comin' of 'em, trunks or hen-
coops, we might. There's somethin' to see, there. That
little bridge leadin' over to the swings and seats across the
river was real pretty and pleasant. And the cars comin'
in an' startin' off, right at the back door, made it lively.
I alwers *did* like to see passin'."

The attitudes inside the blinds were something, at this
moment. Mrs. Lincefo:d, in a spasm of suppressed laughter herself, held her handkerchief to her lips with one
hand, and motioned peremptory silence to the girls with
the other. Jeannie was noiselessly clapping her hands,
and dancing from one toe to the other with delight.
Leslie and Elinor squeezed each other's fingers lightly,
and leaned forward together, their faces brimming over
with fun ; and the former whispered with emphatic pan-
tomime to Mrs. Lineeford, " *If* Mr. Wharne were only
here ! "

" You 've been worried," said the man. " And you 've
ben comin' up to 'em gradooal. You don't take 'em in.
If one of these 'ere hills was set out in our fields to home,
you 'd think it was something more than a hummock, I
guess."

" Well, why ain't they, then ? It 's the best way to put
things where you can see 'em to an advantage. They 're
all in the way of each other here, and don't show for nothing to speak of. Worried ! I guess I hev ben ! I shan't
git over it till I 've got home an' ben settled down a week.

It 's a mercy I 've ever laid eyes agin on that bran-new black alpacky ! "

" Well, p'r'aps the folks felt wuss that lost them stylish-lookin' trunks. I 'll bet they had something more in 'em than black alpackys."

" That don't comfort me none. I 've had *my* tribulation."

" Well, come, don't be grouty, Hannah. We 've got through the wust of it, and if you ain't satisfied, why, we 'll go back to Plymouth again. I can stand it awhile, I guess, if '*t is* four dollars a day."

He had evidently sat still a good while for him, honest man ; and he got up with this, and began to pace up and down, looking at the "hummocks," which signified greater meanings to him than to his wife.

Mrs. Linceford came over and put the window down. It was absolutely necessary to laugh now, however much of further entertainment might be cut off.

Hannah jumped up, electrified, as the sash went down behind her.

" John ! John ! There 's folks in there ! "

" S'pose likely," said John, with quiet relish of amends. " What 's good for me 'ill do for them ! "

V.

"GRIMGRIFFINHOOF won't speak to you to-night," said Jeannie Hadden, after tea, upon the balcony.

She was mistaken. There was something different, still, in Leslie Goldthwaite's look, as she came out under the sunset-light, from the looks that prevailed in the Thoresby group when they too made their appearance. The one moved self-forgetfully, — her consciousness and thought sent forth, not fluttering in her robes and ribbons; with the others there was a little air and bustle, as of people coming into an opera-box in presence of a full house. They said "Lovely!" and "Splendid!" of course, — their little word of applause for the scenic grandeur of mountain and heaven, and then the half of them turned their backs upon it, and commenced talking together about whether waterfalls were really to be given up or not, and of how people were going to look in high-crowned bonnets.

Mrs. Linceford told the "hummux" story to Marmaduke Wharne. The old man laughed till the Thoresby party turned to see.

"But I like one thing," he said. "The woman was honest. Her ' black alpacky ' was most to her, and she owned up to it."

The regular thing being done, outside, the company drifted back, as the shadows fell, to the parlor again. Mrs. Linceford's party moved also, and drifted with the rest. Marmaduke Wharne, quite graciously, walked after. The Lancers was just forming.

"The bear is playing tame and amiable," whispered Jeannie. "But he 'll eat you up, for all that. I would n't trust him. He 's going to watch, to see how wicked you 'll be."

" I shall let him see," replied Leslie, quietly.

"Miss Goldthwaite, you 're for the dance to-night? For the 'bright and kind and pleasant,' eh?" the "bear" said, coming to her side within the room.

"If anybody asks me," answered Leslie, with brave simplicity. "I like dancing — *very* much."

"I 'll find you a partner, then," said Mr. Wharne.

She looked up, surprised; but he was quite in earnest. He walked across the room, and brought back with him a lad of thirteen or so, — well grown for his age, and bright and manly-looking; but only a boy, and a little shy and stiff at first, as boys have to be for a while. Leslie had seen him before, in the afternoon, rolling the balls through a solitary game of croquet; and, afterward, taking his tea by himself at the lower end of the table. He had seemed to belong to nobody, and as yet hardly to have got the "run" of the place.

"This is Master Thayne, Miss Leslie Goldthwaite, and I think he would like to dance, if you please."

Master Thayne made a proper bow, and glanced up at the young girl with a smile lurking behind the diffidence in his face. Leslie smiled outright, and held out her hand.

It was not a brilliant *début*, perhaps. The Haddens had been appropriated by a couple of youths in frock-

coats and orthodox kids, with a suspicion of moustaches;
and one of the Thoresbys had a young captain of cavalry,
with gold bars on his shoulders. Elinor Hadden raised
her pretty eyebrows, and put as much of a mock-miser-
able look into her happy little face as it could hold, when
she found her friend, so paired, at her right hand.

" It's very good of you to stand up with me," said the
boy, simply. " It's awful slow, not knowing anybody."

" Are you here alone ? " asked Leslie.

" Yes; there was nobody to come with me. Oliver
— my brother — will come by and by, and perhaps my
uncle and the rest of them, to meet me where I'm to be,
down among the mountains. We're all broken up this
summer, and I'm to take care of myself."

" Then you don't stay here ? "

" No; I only came this way to see what it was like.
I've got a jolly place engaged for me, at Outledge."

" Outledge ?   Why, we are going there ! "

" Are you?   That's — jolly ! " repeated the boy,
pausing a second for a fresher or politer word, but unable
to supply a synonyme.

" I'm glad you think so," answered Leslie, with her
genuine smile again.

The two had already made up their minds to be
friends. In fact, Master Thayne would hardly have ac-
quiesced in being led up for introduction to any other
young girl in the room. There had been something in
Leslie Goldthwaite's face that had looked kind and sisterly to him. He had no fear of a snub with her; and
these things Mr. Wharne had read, in his behalf, as well.

" He's a queer old fellow, that Mr. Wharne, is n't

5

he ? " pursued Master Thayne, after forward and back, as
he turned his partner to place.   "But he's the only one
that's had anything to say to me, and I like him.   I've
been down to the old mill with him to-day.   Those people " — motioning slightly toward the other set, where
the Thoresbys were dancing — "were down there too.
You'd ought to have seen them look!   Don't they hate
him, though ? "

"Hate him ?   Why should they do that ? "

"O, I don't know.   People feel each other out, I suppose.   And a word of his is as much as a whole preach
of anybody's else.   He says a word now and then, and it
hits."

"Yes," responded Leslie, laughing.

"What *did* you do it for? " whispered Elinor, in
hands across.

"I like him; he's got something to say," returned
Leslie.

"Augusta's looking at you, like a hen after a stray
chicken.   She's all but clucking now."

"Mr. Wharne will tell her."

But Mr. Wharne was not in the room.   He came back
just as Leslie was making her way again, after the
dance, to Mrs. Linceford.

"Will you do a galop with me presently? — if you
don't get a better partner, I mean," said Master Thayne.

"That would n't be much of a promise," answered
Leslie, smiling.   "I will, at any rate; that is, if — after
I've spoken to Mrs. Linceford."

Mr. Wharne came up and said something to young
Thayne, just then; and the latter turned eagerly to Les-

fie. "The telescope's fixed, out on the balcony; and you can see Jupiter and three of his moons! We must make haste, before *our* moon's up."

"Will you go and look, Mrs. Linceford?" asked Mr. Wharne of the lady, as Leslie reached her side.

They went with him, and Master Thayne followed. Jeannie and Elinor and the Miss Thoresbys were doing the inevitable promenade after the dance, — under difficulties.

"Who is your young friend?" inquired Mrs. Linceford, with a shade of doubt in her whisper, as they came out on the balcony.

"Master —— " Leslie began to introduce, but stopped. The name, which she had not been quite certain of, escaped her.

"My name is Dakie Thayne," said the boy, with a bow to the matron.

"Now, Mrs. Linceford, if you'll just sit here," said Mr. Wharne, placing a chair. "I suppose I ought to have come to you first; but it's all right," he added, in a low tone, over her shoulder. "He's a nice boy."

And Mrs. Linceford put her eye to the telescope. "Dakie Thayne! It's a queer name; and yet it seems as if I had heard it before," she said, looking away through the mystic tube into space, and seeing Jupiter with his moons, in a fair round picture framed expressly to her eye; yet sending a thought, at the same time, up and down the lists of a mental directory, trying to place Dakie Thayne among people she had heard of.

"I'll be responsible for the name," answered Marmaduke Wharne.

"'Dakie' is a nickname, of course; but they always call me so, and I like it best," the boy was explaining to Leslie, while they waited in the doorway.

Then her turn came. Leslie had never looked through a telescope upon the stars before. She forgot the galop, and the piano tinkled out its gayest notes un-heard. "It seems like coming all the way back," she said, when she moved away for Dakie Thayne.

Then they wheeled the telescope upon its pivot east-ward, and met our own moon coming up, as if in a grand jealousy, to assert herself within her small domain, and put out faint, far satellites of lordlier planets. They looked upon her mystic, glistening hill-tops, and down her awful craters; and from these they seemed to drop a little, as a bird might, and alight on the earth-moun-tains, looming close at hand, with their huge, rough crests and sides, and sheer escarpments white with nakedness; and so — got home again. Leslie, with her maps and gazetteer, had done no travelling like this.

She would not have cared, if she had known, that Imo-gen Thoresby was looking for her, within, to present, at his own request, the cavalry captain. She did not know in the least, absorbed in her pure enjoyment, that Marma-duke Wharne was deliberately trying her, and confirming his estimate of her, in these very things.

She danced her galop with Dakie Thayne, after she went back. The cavalry captain was introduced, and asked for it. "That was something," as Hans Andersen would say; but "What a goose not to have managed better!" was what Imogen Thoresby thought concerning it, as the gold bars turned themselves away.

Leslie Goldthwaite had taken what came to her, and she had had an innocent, merry time ; she had been glad to be dressed nicely, and to look her best ; — but somehow she had not thought of that much, after all ; the old uncomfortableness had not troubled her to-night.

"*Just to be in better business.* That's the whole of it," she thought to herself, with her head upon the pillow. She put it in words, mentally, in the same off-hand fashion in which she would have spoken it to Cousin Delight. "One must look out for that, and keep at it. *That's* the eyestone-woman's way ; and it's what has kept me from worrying and despising myself to-night. It only happened so, this time ; it was Mr. Wharne, — not I. But I suppose one can always find something, by trying. And the trying — " The rest wandered off into a happy musing ; and the musing merged into a dream.

Object and motive, — the " seeking first " ; she had touched upon that, at last, with a little comprehension of its working.

She liked Dakie Thayne. The next day they saw a good deal of him ; he joined himself gradually, but not obtrusively, to their party ; they included him in their morning game of croquet. This was at her instance ; he was standing aside, not expecting to be counted in, though he had broken off his game of *solitaire*, and driven the balls up to the starting-stake, as they came out upon the ground. The Thoresby set had ignored him, always, being too many already among themselves, — and he was only a boy.

This morning there were only Imogen, and Etty, the

youngest; a walking-party had gone off up the Cherry-Mountain road, and Ginevra was up stairs, packing; for the Thoresbys had also suddenly decided to leave for Outledge on the morrow. Mrs. Thoresby declared, in confidence, to Mrs. Linceford, that "old Wharne would make any house intolerable; and that Jefferson, at any rate, was no place for more than a week's stay." She "would n't have it mentioned in the house, however, that she was going, till the time came, — it made such an ado; and everybody's plans were at loose ends among the mountains, ready to fix themselves to anything at a day's notice; they might have to-morrow's stage loaded to crushing, if they did not take care."

"But I thought Mrs. Devreaux and the Klines were with you," remarked Mrs. Linceford.

"Of our party? O, no indeed; we only fell in with them here."

"Fell in" with them; became inseparable for a week; and now were stealing a march, — *dodging* them, — lest there might be an overcrowding of the stage, and an impossibility of getting outside seats! Mrs. Thoresby was a woman of an imposing elegance and dignity, with her large curls of resplendent gray hair, high up on her temples, her severely-handsome dark eyebrows, and her own perfect, white teeth; yet she could do a shabby thing, you see, — a thing made shabby by its motive. The Devreaux and Klines were only "floating people," boarding about, — not permanently valuable as acquaintances; well enough to know when one met them, — that was all. Mrs. Thoresby had daughters; she was obliged to calculate as to what was worth while. Mrs. Linceford had an elegant establishment in New York; she had young sisters to bring out; there was suitability here; and the girls would naturally find themselves happy together.

Dakie Thayne developed brilliantly at croquet. He and Leslie, with Etty Thoresby, against Imogen and the Haddens, swept triumphantly around the course, and came in to the stake, before there had been even a "rover" upon the other side. Except, indeed, as they were *sent* roving, away off over the bank and down the road, from the sloping, uneven ground, — the most extraordinary field, in truth, on which croquet was ever attempted. But then you cannot expect a level, velvet lawn on the side of a mountain.

"Children always get the best of it at croquet, — when they know anything at all," said Imogen Thoresby, discontentedly, throwing down her mallet. "You 'poked' awfully, Etty."

Etty began an indignant denial; unable to endure the double accusation of being a child, — she, a girl in her fourteenth year, — and of "poking." But Imogen walked away quite unconcernedly, and Jeannie Hadden followed her. These two, as nearest in age, were growing intimate. Ginevra was almost too old, — she was twenty.

They played a four-ball game then; Leslie and Etty against Elinor and Dakie Thayne. But Elinor declared — laughing, all the same, in her imperturbably good-natured way — that not only Etty's pokes were against her, but that Dakie would *not* croquet Leslie's ball down hill. Nothing ever really put Elinor Hadden out, the girls said of her, except when her hair would n't go up; and then it was funny to see her. It was a sunbeam in a

snarl, or a snow-flurry out of a blue sky. This in paren-
thesis, however; it was quite true, as she alleged, that
Dakie Thayne had taken up already that chivalrous attitude toward Leslie Goldthwaite which would not let him
act otherwise than as her loyal knight, even though op-
posed to her at croquet.

"You'll have enough of that boy," said Mrs. Linceford,
when Leslie came in and found her at her window that
overlooked the wickets. "There's nothing like a mascu-
line creature of that age for adoring and monopolizing a
girl two or three years older. He'll make you mend his
gloves, and he'll beg your hair-ribbons for hat-strings;
and when you're not dancing or playing croquet with
him, he'll be after you with some boy-hobby or other,
wanting you to sympathize and help. 'I know their
tricks and their manners.'" But she looked amused and
kind while she threatened, and Leslie only smiled back
and said nothing.

Presently fresh fun gathered in Mrs. Linceford's eyes.
"You're making queer friends, child, do you know, at
the beginning of your travels? We shall have Cocky-
locky, and Turkey-lurky, and Goosie-poosie, and all the
rest of them, before we get much farther. Don't breathe
a word, girls," she went on, turning toward them all, and
brimming over with merriment and mischief, — "but
there's the best joke brewing. It's just like a farce.
Is the door shut, Elinor? And are the Thoresbys gone
up stairs? 'They're going with us, you know? And
there's nothing to be said about it? And it's partly to
get away from Marmaduke Wharne? Well, *he's* going
too. .And it's greatly because they're spoiling the place

for him here. He thinks he'll try Outledge; and there's nothing to be said about that either! And I'm the unhappy depositary of all their complaints and secrets. And if nobody's stopped, they'll all be off in the stage with us to-morrow morning! I couldn't help telling you, for it was too good to keep."

The secrets were secrets through the day; and Mrs. Linceford had her quiet fun, and opportunity for her demure teasing.

"How long since Outledge was discovered and settled? By the moderns, I mean," said Mr. Wharne. "What chance will one really have of quiet there?"

"Well, really, to be honest, Mr. Wharne, I'm afraid Outledge will be just at the rampant stage this summer. It's the second year of anything like general accommodation, and everybody has just heard of it, and it's the knowing and stylish thing to go there. For a week or two it may be quiet; but then there'll be a jam. There'll be hops, and tableaux, and theatricals, of course; interspersed with 'picnicking at the tomb of Jehoshaphat,' or whatever mountain solemnity stands for that. It'll be human nature right over again, be assured, Mr. Wharne."

Yet, somehow, Mr. Wharne would not be frightened from his determination. Until the evening; when plans came out, and good-byes and wonders and lamentations began.

"Yes, we have decided quite suddenly; the girls want to see Outledge, and there's a pleasant party of friends, you know, — one can't always have that. We shall probably fill a stage, — so they will take us through, instead of dropping us at the Crawford House." In this

4

manner Mrs. Thoresby explained to her dear friend, Mrs. Devreaux.

" We shall be quite sorry to lose you all. But it would only have been a day or so longer, at any rate. Our rooms are engaged for the fifteenth, at Saratoga ; we 've very little time left for the mountains, and it would n't be worth while to go off the regular track. We shall probably go down to the Profile on Saturday."

And then — *da capo* — " Jefferson was no place really to *stay* at; you got the whole in the first minute," &c., &c.

" Good night, Mrs. Linceford. I 'm going up to unpack my valise and make myself comfortable again. All things come round, or go by, I find, if one only keeps one's self quiet. But I shall look in upon you at Outledge yet." These were the stairway words of Marmaduke Wharne to-night.

" ' One gets the whole in the first minute ' ! How can they keep saying that ? Look. Elinor, and see if you can tell me where we are ? " was Leslie's cry, as, early next morning, she drew up her window-shade, to look forth — on what ?

Last night had lain there, underneath them, the great basin between Starr King, behind, and the roots of that lesser range, far down, above which the blue Lafayette uprears itself. An enormous valley, filled with evergreen forest, over whose tall pines and cedars one looked, as if they were but juniper and blueberry bushes ; far up above whose heads the real average of the vast mountain-country heaped itself in swelling masses, — miles and miles of beetling height and solid breadth. This morning it was gone ; only the great peaks showed themselves, as a far-oft, cliff-bound shore, or here and there a green island in a vast, vaporous lake. The night-chill had come down among the heights, condensing the warm exhalations of the valley-bosom that had been shone into all day yesterday by the long summer sun ; till, when he lifted himself once more out of the east, sending his leaping light from crest to crest, white fallen clouds were tumbling and wreathing themselves about the knees and against the mighty bosoms of the giants, and at their feet the forest was a sea.

"We must dress, and we must look!" exclaimed Leslie, as the early summons came for them. "O dear! O dear! if we were only like the birds! or if all this would wait till we get down!"

"Please drop the shade just a minute, Les. This glass is in such a horrid light! I don't seem to have but half a face, and I can't tell which is the up-side of that! And — O dear! I've no *time* to get into a fuss!" Elinor had not disdained the beauty and wonder without, but it was, after all, necessary to be dressed, and in a given time ; and a bad light for a looking-glass is such a disastrous thing!

"I've brushed out half my crimps," she said again ; "and my ruffle is basted in wrong side out, and altogether I'm got up *à la furieuse!*" But she laughed before she had done scolding, catching sight of her own exaggerated little frown in the distorting glass, that was unable, with all its malice, to spoil the bright young face when it came to smiles and dimples.

And then Jeannie came knocking at the door. They had spare minutes, after all, and the mists were yet tost

ing in the valley when they went down. They were
growing filmy, and floating away in shining fragments up
over the shoulders of the hills, and the lake was lower
and less, and the emerging green was like the "Thousand Islands."

They waited a little there, in the wide, open door, together, and looked out upon it; and then the Haddens
went round into their sister's room, and Leslie was left
alone in the rare, sweet, early air. The secret joy came
whispering at her heart again ; that there was all this in
the world, and that one need not be utterly dull and
mean, and dead to it; that something in her answered to
the greatness overshadowing her; that it was possible,
sometimes, and that people did reach out into a larger
life than that of self and every-day. How else did the
great mountains draw them to themselves so? But then
she would not always be among the mountains.

And so she stood, drinking in at her eyes all the shifting and melting splendors of the marvellous scene, with
her thought busy, once more, in its own questioning.
She remembered what she had said to Cousin Delight:
"It is all outside. Going, and doing, and seeing, and
hearing, and having. In myself, am I good for any
more, after all?   Or only — a green fig-tree in the sunshine ? "

Why, with that word, did it all flash together for her,
as a connected thing? Her talk that morning, many
weeks ago, that had seemed to ramble so from one irrel-
evant matter to another, — from the parable to her fancy-
travelling, — the scenes and pleasures she had made for
herself, wondering if the real would ever come, — to the

linen-drawer, representing her little feminine absorptions and interests, — and back to the fig-tree again, ending with that word, — "the real living is the urging toward the fruit"? Her day's journey, and the hints of life — narrowed, suffering, working — that had come to her, each with its problem? Marmaduke Wharne's indignant protest against people who "did not know their daily bread," and his insistence upon the *two* things for human creatures to do, — the *receiving* and the giving; the taking from God, in the sunshine, to grow; the ripening into generous uses for others; was it all one, and did it define the whole, and was it identical, in the broadest and highest, with that sublime double command whereon "hang the law and the prophets"?

Something like this passed into her mind and soul, brightening there, like the morning. It seemed, in that glimpse, so clear and gracious, — the truth that had been puzzling her.

Easy, beautiful summer-work; only to be shone upon; to lift up one's branching life, and be — reverently — glad; to grow sweet and helpful and good-giving, in one's turn; — could she not begin to do that? Perhaps — by ever so little; the fruit might be but a berry, yet it might be fair and full, after its kind; and, at least, some little bird might be the better for it. All around her, too, the life of the world that had so troubled her, — who could tell, in the tangle of green, where the good and the gift might ripen and fall? Every little fern-frond has its seed.

Jeannie came behind her again, and called her back to the contradictory phase of self, that, with us all, is almost ready, like Peter, to deny the true. "What are you deep in now, Les?"

"Nothing. Only — we go *down* from here, don't we, Jeannie?"

"Yes. And a very good thing for you, too. You've been in the clouds long enough. I shall be glad to get you to the common level again."

"You've no need to be anxious. I can come down as fast as anybody. *That* is n't the hard thing to do. Let's go in, and get salt-fish and cream for our breakfast."

The Haddens were new to mountain travel; the Thoresbys, literally, were "old stagers"; they were up in the stable-yard before Mrs. Linceford's party came out from the breakfast-room. Dakie Thayne was there too; but that was quite natural for a boy.

They got their outside seats by it, scrambling up before the horses were put to, and sitting there while the hostlers smiled at each other over their work. There was room for two more, and Dakie Thayne took a place; but the young ladies looked askance, for Ginevra had been detained by her mother, and Imogen had hoped to keep a seat for Jeannie, without drawing the whole party after her, and running aground upon politeness. So they drove round to the door.

"First come, first served," cried Imogen, beckoning Jeannie, who happened to be there, looking for her friend. "I've saved a place for you"; — and Jeannie Hadden, nothing loath, as a man placed the mounting-board, sprang up and took it.

Then the others came out. Mrs Thoresby and Mrs

Linceford got inside the vehicle at once, securing comfortable back corner-seats. Ginevra, with Leslie and Elinor, and one or two others too late for their own interest, but quite comprehending the thing to be preferred, lingered while the last trunks went on, hoping for room to be made somehow.

"It's so gay on the top, going down into the villages. There's no fun inside," said Imogen, complacently, settling herself upon her perch.

"Won't there be another stage?"

"Only half-way. This one goes through."

"I'll go half-way on the other, then," said Ginevra.

"This is the best team, and goes on ahead," was the reply.

"You'll be left behind," cried Mrs. Thoresby. "Don't think of it, Ginevra!"

"Can't that boy sit back, on the roof?" asked the young lady.

"That boy" quite ignored the allusion; but presently, as Ginevra moved toward the coach-window to speak with her mother, he leaned down to Leslie Goldthwaite. "I'll make room for *you*," he said.

But Leslie had decided. She could not, with effrontery of selfishness, take the last possible place, — a place already asked for by another. She thanked Dakie Thayne, and, with just one little secret sigh, got into the interior, placing herself by the farther door.

At that moment she missed something. "I've left my brown veil in your room, Mrs. Linceford"; — and she was about to alight again to go for it.

"I'll fetch it," cried Dakie Thayne from overhead,

and, as he spoke, came down, on her side, by the wheel, and, springing around to the house entrance, disappeared up the stairs.

" Ginevra ! " Then there came a laugh and a shout and some crinoline against the forward open corner of the coach, and Ginevra Thoresby was by the driver's side. A little ashamed, in spite of herself, though it was done under cover of a joke ; but " All 's fair among the mountains," somebody said, and " Possession 's nine points," said another, and the laugh was with her, seemingly.

Dakie Thayne flushed up, hot, without a word, when he came out, an instant after.

" I 'm *so* sorry ! " said Leslie, with real regret, accented with honest indignation.

" It 's your place," called out a rough man, who made the third upon the coach-box. " Why don't you stick up for it ? "

The color went down slowly in the boy's face, and a pride came up in his eye. He put his hand to his cap, with a little irony of deference, and lifted it off with the grace of a grown man. " I know it 's my place. But the young lady may keep it — now. *I 'd* rather be a gentleman ! " said Dakie Thayne.

" You 've got the best of it ! " This came from Marmaduke Wharne, as the door closed upon the boy, and the stage rolled down the road toward Cherry Mountain.

There is a " best " to be got out of everything ; but it is neither the best of place or possession, nor the chuck.e of the last word.

VI.

AMONG the mountains, somewhere between the An-
droscoggin and the Saco, — I don't feel bound to tell
you precisely where, and I have only a story-teller's
word to give you for it at all, — lies the little neighborhood of Outledge. An odd corner of a great township
such as they measure off in these wilds, where they take
in, with some eligible " locations " of intervale land, miles
also of pathless forest where the bear and the moose are
wandering still, a pond, perhaps, filling up a basin of
acres and acres in extent, and a good-sized mountain or
two, throw⌐ ↄ to keep off the north-wind, — a corner
cut off, as its name indicates, by the outrunning of a pre-
cipitous ridge of granite, round which a handful of popu-
lation had crept and built itself a group of dwellings, —
this was the spot discovered and seized to themselves
some four or five years since by certain migratory pio-
neers of fashion.

An old two-story farm-house, with four plain rooms of
generous dimensions on each floor, in which the first
delighted summer-party had divided itself, glad and grateful to occupy them double and even treble bedded, had
become the " hotel," with a name up across the gable
of the new wing, — " Giant's-Cairn House," — and the
eight original rooms made into fourteen. The wing was
clapped on by its middle ; rushing out at the front toward
the road to meet the summer-tide of travel as it should
surge by, and hold up to it, arrestively, its singular sign-

4 *   F

board ; the other half as expressively making its bee-line toward the river and the mountain-view at back, — just as each fresh arrival, seeking out the preferable rooms, inevitably did   Behind, upon the other side, an L provided new kitchens ; and over these, within a year, had been carried up a second story, with a hall for dancing, tableaux, theatricals, and travelling jugglers.

Up to this hostelry whirled daily, from the southward, the great six-horse stage ; and from the northward came thrice a week wagons or coaches " through the hills," besides such " extras" as might drive down at any hour of day or night.

Round the smooth curve of broad, level road that skirted the ledges from the upper village pranced four splendid bays ; and after them rollicked an ·wayed, with a perfect delirium of wheels and springs, the great black and yellow-bodied vehicle, like a huge bumble-bee buzzing back with its spoil of a June day to the hive.   The June sunset was golden and rosy upon the hills and cliffs, and Giant's Cairn stood burnished against the eastern blue.   Gay companies, scattered about piazzas and greenswards, stopped in their talk, or their promenades, or their croquet, to watch the arrivals.

" It's stopping at the Green Cottage."

" It's the Haddens.   Their rooms have been waiting since the twenty-third, and all the rest are full."   And two or three young girls dropped mallets and ran over.

" Maud Walcott ! "   " Mattie Shannon ! "

" Jeannie ! "   " Nell ! "

" How came *you* here ? "

" We 've been here these ten days, — looking for you the last three."

" Why, I can't take it in !   I 'm so surprised ! "

" Is n't it jolly, though ? "

. " Miss Goldthwaite, — Miss Walcott.   Miss Shannon, — Miss Goldthwaite. — My sister, Mrs. Linceford."

" *Me voici !* "   And a third came up, suddenly, laying a hand upon each of the Haddens from behind.

" You, Sin Saxon !   How many more ? "

" We 're coming, Father Abraham !   All of us, nearly ; three hundred thousand more — or less ; half the Routh girls, with Madam to the fore ! "

" And we 've got all the farther end of the wing down stairs, — the garden bedrooms ; you 've no idea how scrumptious it is !   You must come over after tea, and see."

" Not all, Mattie ; you forget the solitary spinster."

" No, I don't ; who ever does ?   But can't you ignore her for once ?

" Or let a fellow speak in the spirit of prophecy ? " said Sin Saxon.   " We 're sure to get the better of Gray-wacke, and why not anticipate ? "

" Graywacke ? " said Jeannie Hadden.   " Is that a name ?   It sounds like the side of a mountain."

" And acts like one," rejoined Sin Saxon.   " Won't budge.   But it is n't her name, exactly ; only Saxon for Craydocke ; suggestive of obstinacy and the Old Silu-rian.   An ancient maiden who infests our half the wing. We 've got all the rooms but hers, and we 're bound to get her out.   She 's been there three years, in the same spot, — went in with the lath and plaster, — and its *time*

she started. Besides, have n't I got manifest destiny on
my side? Ain't I a Saxon?" Sin Saxon tossed up a
merry, bewitching, saucy glance out of her blue, starlike
eyes, that shone under a fair, low brow touched and
crowned lightly with the soft haze of gold-brown locks
frizzed into a delicate mistiness after the ruling fashion of
the hour.

"What a pretty thing she is!" said Mrs. Linceford,
when, seeing her busy with her boxes, and the master of
the house approaching to show the new arrivals to their
rooms, Sin Saxon and her companions flitted away as they
had come, with a few more sentences of bright girl-non-
sense flung back at parting. "And a witty little minx,
as well. Where did you know her, Jeannie? And what
sort of a satanic name is that you call her by?"

"Just suits such a mischief, does n't it? Short for
Asenath, — it was always her school-name. She 's just
finished her last year at Madam Routh's ; she came there
soon after we did. It 's a party of the graduates, and
some younger ones left with Madam for the long holi-
days, that she 's travelling with. I wonder if she is n't
sick of her life, though, by this time! Fancy those girls,
Nell, with a whole half-wing of the hotel to themselves,
and Sin Saxon in the midst!"

"Poor 'Graywacke' in the midst, you mean," said
Nell.

"Like a respectable old grimalkin at the mercy of a
crowd of boys and a tin kettle," added Jeannie, laughing.

"I 've no doubt she's a very nice person, too. I only
hope, if I come across her, I may n't call her Graywacke
to her face," said Mrs. Linceford.

"Just what you 'll be morally sure to do, Augusta!"

With this, they had come up the staircase and along a narrow passage leading down between a dozen or so of small bedrooms on either side, — for the Green Cottage also had run out its addition of two stories since summer guests had become many and importunate, — and stood now where three open doors, one at the right and two at the left, invited their entrance upon what was to be their own especial territory for the next two months. From one side they looked up the river along the face of the great ledges, and caught the grandeur of far-off Washington, Adams, and Madison, filling up the northward end of the long valley. The aspect of the other was toward the frowning glooms of Giant's Cairn close by, and broadened then down over the pleasant subsidence of the southern country to where the hills grew less, and fair, small, modest peaks lifted themselves just into blue height and nothing more, smiling back with a contented deference toward the mightier majesties, as those who might say, — "We do our gentle best ; it is not yours ; yet we too are mountains, though but little ones." From underneath spread the foreground of green, brilliant intervale, with the river flashing down between margins of sand and pebbles in the midst.

Here they put Leslie Goldthwaite ; and here, somehow, her first sensation, as she threw back her blinds to let in all the twilight for her dressing, was a feeling of half relief from the strained awe and wonder of the last few days. Life would not seem so petty here as in the face of all that solemn stateliness. There was a reaction of respite and repose. And why not ? The great emo

tions are not meant to come to us daily in their unquali-
fied strength. God knows how to dilute his elixirs for
the soul. His fine, impalpable air, spread round the
earth, is not more cunningly mixed from pungent gases
for our hourly breath, than life itself is thinned and toned
that we may receive and bear it.

Leslie wondered if it were wrong that the high mountain fervor let itself go from her so soon and easily ; that
the sweet pleasantness of this new resting-place should
come to her *as* a rest ; that the laughter and frolic of the
school-girls made her glad with such sudden sympathy
and foresight of enjoyment ; that she should have " come
down " all the way from Jefferson in Jeannie's sense, and
that she almost felt it a comfortable thing herself not to
be kept always " up in the clouds."

Sin Saxon, as they called her, was so bright and odd
and fascinating ; was there any harm — because no special, obvious good — in that ?   There was a little twinge
of doubt, remembering poor Miss Craydocke ; but that
had seemed pure fun, not malice, after all, — and it was,
hearing Sin Saxon tell it, very funny. She could imagine
the life they led the quiet lady, — yet, if it were quite
intolerable, why did she remain ?   Perhaps, after all, she
saw through the fun of it. And I think, myself, perhaps
she did.

The Marie Stuart net went on to-night ; and then
such a pretty muslin, white, with narrow, mode-brown
stripes, and small, bright leaves dropped over them, as if
its wearer had stood out under a maple-tree in October,
and all the tiniest and most radiant bits had fallen and
fastened themselves about her. And, last of all, with her

little hooded cape of scarlet cashmere over her arm, she
went down to eat cream-biscuit and wood-strawberries
for tea. Her summer life began with a charming fresh-
ness and dainty delight.

There were pleasant voices of happy people about them
in hall and open parlor, as they sat at their late repast.
Everything seemed indicative of abundant coming enjoyment ; and the girls chatted gayly of all they had already
discovered or conjectured, and began to talk of the ways
of the place and the sojourners in it, quite like old *ha-
bituées*.

It was even more delightful yet, strolling out when tea
was over, and meeting the Routh party again half-way
between the cottage and the hotel, and sauntering on
with them, insensibly, till they found themselves on the
wide wing-piazza, upon which opened the garden bedrooms, and being persuaded after all to sit down since
they had got there, though Mrs. Linceford had demurred
at a too hasty rushing over, as new-comers, to begin
visits.

" O, nobody knows when they *are* called upon here, or
who comes first," said Mattie Shannon. " We generally
receive half-way across the green, and it 's a chance
which turns back, or whether we get near either house
again or not. Houses don't signify, except when it
rains."

" But it just signifies that you should see how mag-
nificently we have settled ourselves for nights, and dressing, and when it *does* rain," said Sin Saxon, throwing
back a door behind her, that stood a little ajar. It opened
directly into a small apartment, half parlor and half

dressing-room, from which doors showed others, on either side, furnished as sleeping-rooms.

"It was Maud Walcott's, between the Arnalls' and mine; but, what with our trunks, and our beds, and our crinolines, and our towel-stands, we wanted a Bowditch's Navigator to steer clear of the reefs, and something was always getting knocked over; so, one night, we were seized simultaneously with an idea. We'd make a boudoir of this for the general good, and forthwith we fell upon the bed, and amongst us got it down. It was the greatest fun! We carried the pieces and the mattresses all off ourselves up to the attic, after ten o'clock, and we gave the chambermaid a dollar next morning, and nobody's been the wiser since. And then we walked to the upper village and bought that extraordinary chintz, and frilled and cushioned our trunks into ottomans, and curtained the dress-hooks; and Lucinda got us a rocking-chair, and Maud came in with me to sleep, and we kept our extra pillows, and we should be comfortable as queens if it was n't for Graywacke."

"Now, Sin Saxon, you know Graywacke is just the life of the house. What would such a parcel of us do, if we had n't something to run upon?"

"Only I'm afraid I shall get tired of it at last. She bears it so. It is n't exactly saintliness, nor Graywacke-iness, but it seems sometimes as if she took a quiet kind of fun out of it herself, — as if she were somehow laughing at us, after all, in her sleeve; and if she is, she's got the biggest end. *She's* bright enough."

"Don't we tree-toad her within an inch of her life, though, when we come home in the wagons at night? I

should n't think she could stand that long. I guess she
wants all her beauty-sleep. And Kate Arnall can tu-
whit, tu-whoo! equal to Tennyson himself, or any great
white *American* owl."

"Yes, but what do you think? As true as I live, I
heard her answer back the other night with such a sly
little 'Katy-did! she did! she did!' I thought at first
it actually came from the great elm-trees. O, she 's been
a girl once, you may depend; and has n't more than half
got over it either. But wait till we have our 'howl'!"

What a "howl" was, superlative to "tree-toading,"
"owl-hooting," and other divertisements, did not appear
at this time; for a young man did, approaching from the
front of the hotel, and came up to the group on the piazza
with the question, "At what time do we set off for
Feather-Cap to-morrow?"

"O, early, Mr. Scherman; by nine o'clock."

"Earlier than you 'll be ready," said Frank Scherman's sister, one of the "Routh" girls also.

"I sha'n't have any crimps to take down, that 's one
thing," Frank answered. And Sin Saxon, glancing at
his handsome waving hair, whispered saucily to Jeannie
Hadden, "I don't more than half believe that, either";
— then, aloud, "You must join the party too, girls, by
the way. It 's one of the nicest excursions here. We 've
got two wagons, and they 'll be full; but there 's Holden's 'little red' will take six, and I don't believe anybody has spoken for it. Mr. Scherman! would n't it
make you happy to go and see?"

"Most intensely!" and Frank Scherman bowed a low,
graceful bow, settling back into his first attitude, how

ever, as one who could quite willingly resign himself to his present comparative unhappiness awhile longer.

"Where is Feather-Cap?" asked Leslie Goldthwaite.

"It's the mountain you see there, peeping round the shoulder of Giant's Cairn; a comfortable little rudiment of a mountain, just enough for a primer-lesson in climbing. Don't you see how the crest drops over on one side, and that scrap of pine — which is really a huge gaunt thing a hundred years old — slants out from it with just a tuft of green at the very tip, like an old feather stuck in jauntily?"

"And the pine-woods round the foot of the Cairn are lovely," said Maud.

"Oh!" cried Leslie, drawing a long breath, as if their spicy smell were already about her, "there is nothing I delight in so as pines!"

"You'll have your fill to-morrow, then; for it's ten miles through nothing else, and the road is like a carpet with the soft brown needles."

"I hope Augusta won't be too tired to feel like going," said Elinor.

"We had better ask her soon, then; she is looking this way now. We ought to go, Sin; we've got all our settling to do for the night."

"We'll walk over with you," said Sin Saxon. "Then we shall have done up all the preliminaries nicely. We called on you — before you were off the stage-coach; you've returned it; and now we'll pay up and leave you owing us one. Come, Mr. Scherman; you'll be so far on your way to Holden's, and perhaps inertia will carry you through."

But a little girl presently appeared, running from the hotel portico at the front, as they came round to view from thence. Madam Routh was sitting in the open hall with some newly arrived friends, and sent one of her lambs, as Sin called them, to say to the older girls that she preferred they should not go away again to-night.

"'Ruin seize thee, Routh—less king!'" quoted Sin Saxon, with an absurd air of declamation. "''T was ever thus from childhood's hour,'—and now, just as we thought childhood's hour was comfortably over,—that the clock had struck one, and down we might run, hickory, dickory, dock,—behold the lengthened sweetness long drawn out of school rule in vacation, even before the very face and eyes of Freedom on her mountain heights! Well, we must go, I suppose. Mr. Scherman, you'll have to represent us to Mrs. Linceford, and persuade her to join us to Feather-Cap. And be sure you get the 'little red'!"

"It'll be all the worse for Graywacke, if we're kept in and sent off early," she continued, *sotto voce*, to her companions, as they turned away. "My! what *has* that boy got?"

After all this, I wonder if you would n't just like to look in at Miss Craydocke's room with me, who can give you a pass anywhere within the geography of my story?

She came in here "with the lath and plaster," as Sin Saxon had said. She had gathered little comforts and embellishments about her from summer to summer, until the room had a home-cheeriness, and even a look of luxury, contrasted with the bare dormitories around it. ' · er the straw matting, that soon grows shabby in a hotel, she had laid a large, nicely-bound square of soft, green carpet, in a little mossy pattern, that covered the middle of the floor, and was held tidily in place by a foot of the bedstead and two forward ones each of the table and washstand. On this little green stood her Shaker rocking-chair and a round white-pine light-stand with her work-basket and a few books. Against the wall hung some white-pine shelves with more books, — quite a little circulating library they were for invalids and read-out people, who came to the mountains, like foolish virgins, with scant supply of the oil of literature for the feeding of their brain-lamps. Besides these, there were engravings and photographs in *passe-partout* frames, that journeyed with her safely in the bottoms of her trunks. Also, the wall itself had been papered, at her own cost and providing, with a pretty pale-green hanging; and there were striped muslin curtains to the window, over which were caught the sprays of some light, wandering vine that sprung from a low-suspended terra cotta vase between.

She had everything pretty about her, this old Miss Craydocke. How many people do, that have not a bit of outward prettiness themselves! Not one cubit to the stature, not one hair white or black, can they add or change ; and around them grow the lilies in the glory of Solomon, and a frosted leaf or a mossy twig, that they can pick up from under their feet and bring home from the commonest walk, comes in with them, bearing a brightness and a grace that seems sometimes almost like a satire ! But in the midst grows silently the century-plant of the soul, absorbing to itself hourly that which feeds the beauty of the lily and the radiance of the leaf, — waiting only for the hundred years of its shrouding to be over!

Miss Craydocke never came in from the woods and rocks without her trophies. Rare, lovely mosses, and bits of most delicate ferns, maiden-hair and lady-bracken, tiny trails of wintergreen and arbutus, filled a great shallow Indian china dish upon her bureau-top, and grew, in their fairy fashion, in the clear, soft water she kept them freshened with.

Shining scraps of mountain minerals, — garnets and bright-tinted quartz and beryls, heaped artistically, rather than scientifically, on a base of jasper and malachite and dark basalt and glistening spar and curious fossils, — these not gathered by any means in a single summer or in ordinary ramblings, but treasured long, and standing, some of them, for friendly memories — balanced on the one side a like grouping of shells and corals and sea-mosses on the other, upon a broad bracket-mantel put up over a little corner fireplace; for Miss Craydocke's room, joining the main house, took the benefit of one of its old chimneys.

Above or about the pictures lay mossy, gnarled, and twisted branches, gray and green, framing them in a forest arabesque; and great pine cones, pendent from their boughs, crowned and canopied the mirror.

"What *do* you keep your kindling-wood up there for?" Sin Saxon had asked, with a grave, puzzled face, coming in, for pure mischief, on one of her frequent and ingenious errands.

"Why, where should I put a pile of wood or a basket?

There 's no room for things to lie round here ; you have
to hang everything up ! " — was Miss Craydocke's answer, quick as a flash, her eyes twinkling comically with
appreciation of the fun.

And Sin Saxon had gone away and told the girls that
the old lady knew how to feather her nest better than
any of them, and was sharp enough at a peck, too, upon
occasion.

She found her again, one morning, sitting in the midst
of a pile of homespun, which she was cutting up with
great shears into boys' blouses.

"There ! that 's the noise that has disturbed me so ! "
cried the girl. "I thought it was a hay-cutter, or a plan-
ing-machine, or that you had got the asthma awfully. I
could n't write my letter for listening to it, and came
round to ask what *was* the matter ! — Miss Craydocke, I
don't see why you keep the door bolted on your side. It
is n't any more fair for you than for me ; and I 'm sure
I do all the visiting. Besides, it 's dangerous. What if
anything should happen in the night ? I could n't get in
to help you. Or there might be a fire in our room, —
I 'm sure I expect nothing else. We boiled eggs in the
Etna the other night, and got too much alcohol in the
saucer ; and then, in the midst of the blaze and excitement, what should Madam Routh do but come knocking
at the door ! Of course we had to put it in the closet,
and there were all our muslin dresses, — that were n't
hanging on the hooks in Maud's room ! I assure you I
felt like the man sitting on the safety-valve, standing
with my back against the door, and my clothes spread
out for fear she would see the flash under the crack !

For we 'd nothing else but moonlight in the room. —
But now tell me, please, what are all these things? Meal-
bags?"

"Do you really want to know?"

"Of course I do. Now that I 've got over my fright
about your strangling with the asthma — those shears did
wheeze so! — my curiosity is all alive again."

"I 've a cousin down in North Carolina teaching the
little freedmen."

"And she 's to have all these sacks to tie the naughty
ones up in? What a bright idea! And then to whip
them with rods as the Giant did his crockery, I suppose?
Or perhaps — they can't be petticoats! Won't she be
warm, though?"

"May be, if you were to take one and sew up the
seams, you would be able to satisfy yourself."

"I? Why, I never *could* put anything together! I
tried once, with a pair of hospital drawers, and they were
like Sam Hyde's dog, that got cut in two, and clapped
together again in a hurry, two legs up, and two legs
down. Miss Craydocke, why don't *you* go down among
the freedmen? You have n't half a sphere up here.
Nothing but Hobbs's Location, and the little Hoskinses."

"I can't organize and execute. Letitia can. It 's her
gift. I can't do great things. I can only just carry round
my little cup of cold water."

"But it gets so dreadfully joggled in such a place as
this! Don't we girls disturb you, Miss Craydocke? I
should think you 'd be quieter in the other wing, or up
stairs."

"Young folks are apt to think that old folks ought to

go a story higher. But we 're content, and they must put up with us, until the proprietor orders a move."

"Well, good by. But if ever you do smell smoke in the night, you 'll draw your bolt the first thing, won't you ?"

This evening, — upon which we have offered you your pass, reader, — Miss Craydocke is sitting with her mosquito bar up, and her candle alight, finishing some pretty thing that daylight has not been long enough for. A flag basket at her feet holds strips and rolls of delicate birch-bark, carefully split into filmy thinness, and heaps of star-mosses, cup-mosses, and those thick and crisp with clustering brown spires, as well as sheets of lichen silvery and pale green; and on the lap-board across her knees lies her work, — a graceful cross in perspective, put on card-board in birch shaded from faint buff to bistre, dashed with the detached lines that seem to have quilted the tree-teguments together. Around the foot of the cross rises a mound of lovely moss-work in relief, with feathery filaments creeping up and wreathing about the shaft and thwart-beam. Miss Craydocke is just dotting in some bits of slender coral-headed stems among little brown mushrooms and chalices, as there comes a sudden, imperative knocking at the door of communication, or defence, between her and Sin Saxon.

"You must just open this time, if you please ! I 've got my arms full, and I could n't come round."

Miss Craydocke slipped her lap-board — work and all — under her bureau, upon the floor, for safety; and then, with her quaint, queer expression, in which curiosity, pluckiness, and a foretaste of amusement mingled so as to

drive out annoyance, pushed back her bolt, and presented herself to the demand of her visitor, much as an un-daunted man might fling open his door at the call of a mob.

Sin Saxon stood there, in the light of the good lady's candle, making a pretty picture against the dim back-ground of the unlighted room beyond. Her fair hair was tossed, and her cheeks flushed ; her blue eyes bright with sauciness and fun. In her hands, or across her arms, rather, she held some huge, uncouth thing, that was not to the last degree dainty-smelling, either ; something con-glomerated rudely upon a great crooked log or branch, which, glanced at closer, proved to be a fragment of gray old pine. Sticks and roots and bark, straw and grass and locks of dirty sheep's-wool, made up its bulk and its unti-diness ; and this thing Sin held out with glee, declaring she had brought a real treasure to add to Miss Cray-docke's collection.

"Such a chance!" she said, coming in. "One mightn't have another in a dozen years. I have just given Jimmy Wigley a quarter for it, and he'd just all but broken his neck to get it. It's a real crow's nest. Corvinus some-thing-else-us, I suppose. Where will you have it. I'm going to nail it up for you myself. Won't it make a nice contrast to the humming-bird's? Over the bed, shall I? But then, if it *should* drop down on your nose, you know ! I think the corner over the fireplace will be best. Yes, we'll have it right up perpendicular, in the angle. The branch twists a little, you see, and the nest will run out with its odds and ends like an old banner. Might I push up the washstand to get on to?"

"Suppose you lay it *in* the fireplace ? It will just rest nicely across those evergreen boughs, and — be in the current of ventilation outward."

" Well, that's an idea, to be sure. — Miss Craydocke ! " — Sin Saxon says this in a sudden interjectional way, as if it were with some quite fresh idea, — " I 'm certain you play chess ! "

" You 're mistaken. I don't."

" You would, then, by intuition. Your counter-moves are — so — triumphant. Why, it 's really an ornament !" With a little stress and strain that made her words interjectional, she had got it into place, thrusting one end up the throat of the chimney, and lodging the crotch that held the nest upon the stems of fresh pine that lay across the andirons ; and the " odds and ends," in safe position, and suggesting neither harm nor unsuitableness, looked unique and curious, and not so ugly.

" It 's really an ornament ! " repeated Sin, shaking the dust off her dress.

" As you expected, of course," replied Miss Craydocke.

" Well, I was n't — not to say — confident. I was afraid it might n't be much but scientific. But now — if you don't forget and light a fire under it some day, Miss Craydocke ! "

" I sha'n't forget ; and I'm very much obliged, really. Perhaps by and by I shall put it in a rough box and send it to a nephew of mine, with some other things, for his collection."

" Goodness, Miss Craydocke ! They won't express it. They 'll think it 's an infernal machine, or a murder !

But it's disposed of for the present, any way. The truth was, you know, twenty-five cents is a kind of cup of cold water to Jimmy Wigley, and then there was the fun of bringing it in, and I did n't know anybody but you to offer it to; I 'm so glad you like it; the girls thought you would n't. Perhaps I can get you another, or something else as curious, some day, — a moose's horns, or a bear-skin; there 's no knowing. But now — apropos of the nest — I 've a crow to *pick* with you. You gave me horrible dreams all night, the last time I came to see you. I don't know whether it was your little freedmen's meal-bags, or Miss Letitia's organizing and executive genius, or the cup of cold water you spoke of, or — it 's just occurred to me — the fuss I had over my waterfall that day, trying to make it into a melon; but I had the most extraordinary time endeavoring to pay you a visit. Down South, it was, and there you were, organizing and executing, after all, on the most tremendous scale, some kind of freedmen's institution. You were explaining to me and showing me all sorts of things, in such enormous bulk and extent and number! First I was to see your stables, where the cows were kept. A trillion of cows! — that was what you told me. And on the way we went down among such wood-piles! — whole forests cut up into kindlings and built into solid walls that reached up till the sky looked like a thread of blue sewing-silk between. And presently we came to a kind of opening and turned off to see the laundry (Mrs. Lisplin had just brought home my things at bedtime) ; and *there* was a place to do the world's washing in, or bleach out all the Ethiopians! Tubs like the hold of the Great Eastern, and spouts coming into them

like the Staubbach! Clothes-lines like a parade-ground
of telegraphs, fields like prairies, snow-patched, as far as
you could see, with things laid out to whiten! And suddenly we came to what was like a pond of milk, with
crowds of negro women stirring it with long poles; and
all at once something came roaring behind and you called
to me to jump aside, — that the hot water was let on to
make the starch; and down it rushed, a cataract like
Niagara, in clouds of steam! And then — well, it changed
to something else, I suppose; but it was after that fashion
all night long, and the last I remember, I was trying to
climb up the Cairn with a cup of cold water set on atilt
at the crown of my head, which I was to get to the sky-
parlor without spilling a drop!"

"Nobody's brain but yours would have put it together
like that," said Miss Craydocke, laughing till she had to
feel for her pocket-handkerchief to wipe away the tears.

"Don't cry, Miss Craydocke," said Sin Saxon, changing suddenly to the most touching tone and expression
of regretful concern. "I did n't mean to distress you.
I don't think anything is really the matter with my
brain!"

"But I 'll tell you what it is," she went on presently,
in her old manner, "I am in a dreadful way with that
waterfall, and I wish you 'd lend me one of your caps, or
advise me what to do. It's an awful thing when the
fashion alters, just as you 've got used to the last one.
You can't go back, and you don't dare to go forward. I
wish hair was like noses, born in a shape, without giving
you any responsibility. But we do have to finish our
selves, and that 's just what makes us restless."

"You have n't come to the worst yet," said Miss Craydocke, significantly.

"What do you mean? What is the worst? Will it come all at once, or will it be broken to me ? "

"It will be broken, and *that's* the worst. One of these years you 'll find a little thin spot coming, may be, and spreading, over your forehead or on the top of your head; and it 'll be the fashion to comb the hair just so as to show it off, and make it worse; and for a while that 'll be your thorn in the flesh. And then you 'll begin to wonder why the color is n't so bright as it used to be, but looks dingy, all you can do to it; and again, after a while, some day, in a strong light, you 'll see there are white threads in it, and the rest is fading; and so by degrees, and the degrees all separate pains, you 'll have to come to it and give up the crown of your youth, and take to scraps of lace and muslin, or a front, as I did a dozen years ago."

Sin Saxon had no sauciness to give back for that; it made her feel all at once that this old Miss Craydocke had really been a girl too, with golden hair like her own, perhaps, — and not so very far in the past either but that a like space in her own future could picture itself to her mind; and something, quite different in her mood from ordinary, made her say, with even an unconscious touch of reverence in her voice, — " I wonder if I shall bear it, when it comes, as well as you ! "

"There 's a recompense," said Miss Craydocke. "You 'll have got it all then. You 'll know there 's never a fifty or a sixty years that does n't hold the tens and the twenties."

"I 've found out something," said Sin Saxon, as she came back to the girls again. "A picked-up dinner argues a fresh one some time. You can't have cold roast mutton unless it has once been hot!" And never a word more would she say to explain herself.

VII.

THE "little red" was at the door of the Green Cottage. Frank Scherman had got the refusal of it the
night before, and early in the morning Madam Routh's
compliments had come to Mrs. Linceford, with the request, in all the form that mountain usage demanded,
that she and the young ladies would make part of the
expedition for the day.

Captain Jotham Green, host and proprietor, stood himself at the horses' heads. The Green Cottage, you perceive, had double right to its appellation. It was both
baptismal and hereditary, surname and given name, —
given with a coat of fresh, pale, pea-green paint that had
been laid upon it within the year, and had communicated
a certain tender, newly-sprouted, May-morning expression
to the old centre and its outshoots.

Mrs. Green, within, was generously busy with biscuits,
cold chicken, doughnuts fried since sunrise, and coffee
richly compounded with cream and sugar, which a great
tin can stood waiting to receive and convey, and which
was at length to serve as cooking utensil in reheating upon
the fire of coals the picnickers would make up under the
very tassel of Feather-Cap.

The great wagons were drawn up also before the piazza
of the hotel; and between the two houses flitted the excursionists, full of the bright enthusiasm of the setting off,
which is the best part of a jaunt, invariably.

Leslie Goldthwaite, in the hamadryad costume, just

aware — which it was impossible for her to help — of its exceeding prettiness, and of glances that recognized it, pleased with a mixture of pleasures, was on the surface of things once more, taking the delight of the moment with a young girl's innocent abandonment. It was nice to be received so among all these new companions; to be evidently, though tacitly, *voted* nice, in the way girls have of doing it; to be launched at once into the beginning of apparently exhaustless delights; — all this was superadded to the first and underlying joy of merely being alive and breathing, this superb summer morning, among these forests and hills.

Sin Saxon, whatever new feeling of half sympathy and respect had been touched in her toward Miss Craydocke the night before, in her morning mood was all alive again to mischief. The small, spare figure of the lady appeared at the side-door, coming out briskly toward them along the passage, just as the second wagon filled up and was ready to move.

I did not describe Miss Craydocke herself when I gave you the glimpse into her room. There was not much to describe; and I forgot it in dwelling upon her surroundings and occupations. In fact, she extended herself into these, and made you take them involuntarily and largely into the account in your apprehension of her. Some people seem to have given them at the outset a mere germ of personality like this, which must needs widen itself out in like fashion to be felt at all. Her mosses and minerals, her pressed leaves and flowers, her odds and ends of art and science and prettiness which she gathered about her, her industries and benevolences, — these were herself. Out of these she was only a little elderly thread-paper of a woman, of no apparent account among crowds of other people, and with scarcely enough of bodily bulk or presence to take any positive foothold anywhere.

What she might have seemed, in the days when her hair was golden, and her little figure plump, and the very unclassical features rounded and rosy with the bloom and grace of youth, was perhaps another thing; but now, with her undeniable "front," and cheeks straightened into lines that gave you the idea of her having slept all night upon both of them, and got them into longitudinal wrinkles that all day was never able to wear out; above all, with her curious little nose, (that was the exact expression of it,) sharply and suddenly thrusting itself among things in general from the middle plane of her face with slight preparatory hint of its intention, — you would scarcely charge her, upon suspicion, with any embezzlement or making away of charms intrusted to her keeping in the time gone by.

This morning, moreover, she had somehow given herself a scratch upon the tip of this odd, investigating member; and it blushed for its inquisitiveness under a scrap of thin pink adhesive plaster.

Sin Saxon caught sight of her as she came. "Little Miss Netticoat!" she cried, just under her breath, "*With* a fresh petticoat, *and* a red nose!" — Then, changing her tone with her quotation, —

> "'Wee, modest, crimson-tippèd flower,
> Thou 'st met me in a luckless hour!'

Thou always dost! What *hast* thou gone and got thyself up so for, just as I was almost persuaded to be good?

5 *

Now — *can* I help that?" And she dropped her folded
hands in her lap, exhaled a little sigh of vanquished
goodness, and looked round appealingly to her companions.

"It's only," said Miss Craydocke, reaching them a
trifle out of breath, "this little parcel, — something I
promised to Prissy Hoskins, — and *would* you just go
round by the Cliff and leave it for me?"

"O, I'm afraid of the Cliff!" cried Florrie Arnall.
"Creggin's horses backed there the other day. It's
horribly dangerous."

"It's three quarters of a mile round," suggested the
driver.

"The 'little red' might take it. They'll go faster
than we, or can, if they try," said Mattie Shannon.

"The 'little red''s just ready," said Sin Saxon.
"You need n't laugh. That was n't a pun. But O
Miss Craydocke!" — and her tone suggested the mischievous apropos, — "what *can* you have been doing to your
nose?"

"O yes!" — Miss Craydocke had a way of saying "O
yes!" — "It was my knife slipped as I was cutting a bit
of cord, in a silly fashion, up toward my face. It's a.
mercy my nose served to save my eyes."

"I suppose that's partly what noses are for," said Sin
Saxon, gravely. "Especially when you follow them,
and 'go it blind.'"

"It was a piece of good luck, too, after all," said Miss
Craydocke, in her simple way, never knowing, or choos-
ing to know, that she was snubbed or quizzed. "Looking for a bit of plaster, I found my little parcel of traga-

canth that I wanted so the other day.   It's queer how
things turn up."

" Excessively queer," said Sin, solemnly, still looking
at the injured feature.   " But as you say, it's all for the
best, after all.   ' There *is* a divinity that shapes our ends,
rough-hew them how we will.'   Hiram, we might as
well drive on.   I'll take the parcel, Miss Craydocke.
We'll get it there somehow, going or coming."

The wagon rolled off, veils and feathers taking the wind
bravely, and making a gay moving picture against the
dark pines and gray ledges. as it glanced along.   Sin
Saxon tossed Miss Craydocke's parcel into the "little
red" as they passed it by, taking the road in advance,
giving a saucy word of command to Jim Holden, which
transferred the charge of its delivery to him, and calling
out a hurried explanation to the ladies over her shoulder
that "it would take them round the Cliff, — the most
wonderful point in all Outledge ; up and down the whole
length of New Hampshire they could see from there, if
their eyes were good enough!"   And so they were
away.

Miss Craydocke turned back into the house, not a whit
discomfited, and with not so much as a contrasting sigh
in her bosom or a rankle in her heart.   On the contrary,
a droll twinkle played among the crow's-feet at the corners of her eyes.   They could not hurt her, these merry
girls, meaning nothing but the moment's fun, nor cheat
her of her quiet share of the fun either.

Up above, out of a window over the piazza roof, looked
two others, young girls, — one of them at least, — also,
upon the scene of the setting-off.

I cannot help it that a good many different people will get into my short story. They get into a short time, in such a summer holiday, and so why not? At any rate, I must tell you about these Josselyns.

These two had never in all their lives been away pleasuring before. They had nobody but each other to come with now. Susan had been away a good deal in the last two years, but it had not been pleasuring. Martha was some five or six years the younger. She had a pretty face, yet marked, as it is so sad to see the faces of the young, with lines and loss, — lines that tell of cares too early felt, and loss of the first fresh, redundant bloom, that such lines bring.

They sat a great deal at this window of theirs. It was a sort of instinct and habit with them, and it made them happier than almost anything else, — sitting at a window together. It was home to them, because at home they lived so, — life and duty were so framed in for them, — in one dear, old window-recess. Sometimes they thought that it would be heaven to them by and by. That such a seat, and such a quiet, happy outlook, they should find kept for them together, in the Father's mansion, up above.

At home, it was up three flights of stairs, in a tall, narrow city house, of which the lower floors overflowed with young, boisterous half brothers and sisters, — the tide not seldom rising and inundating their own retreat, — whose delicate mother, not more than eight years older than her eldest step-daughter, was tied hand and foot to her nursery, with a baby on her lap, and the two or three next above with hands always to be washed, disputes and amusements always to be settled, small morals to be enforced, and clean calico tyers to be incessantly put on.

And Susan and Martha sat up stairs and made the tyers.

Mr. Josselyn was a book-keeper, with a salary of eighteen hundred dollars, and these seven children. And Susan and Martha were girls of fair culture, and womanly tastes, and social longings. How does this seem to you, young ladies, and what do you think of their up-stairs life together, you who calculate, if you calculate at all, whether five hundred dollars may carry you respectably through your half-dozen city assemblies, where you shine in silk and gossamer, of which there will not be "a dress in the room that cost less than seventy-five dollars," and come home, after the dance, "a perfect rag"?

Two years ago, when you were perhaps performing in tableaux for the "benefit of the Sanitary," these two girls had felt the great enthusiasm of the time lay hold of them in a larger way. Susan had a friend — a dear old intimate of school-days, now a staid woman of eight-and-twenty — who was to go out in yet maturer companionship into the hospitals. And Susan's heart burned to go. But there were all the little tyers, and the A B C's, and the faces and fingers.

"I can do it for a while," said Martha, "without you." Those two words held the sacrifice. "Mamma is so nicely this summer, and by and by Aunt Lucy may come, perhaps. I can do *quite* well."

So Martha sat, for months and months, in the up-stairs window alone. There were martial marchings in the streets beneath; great guns thundered out rejoicings;

flags filled the air with crimson and blue, like an aurora; she only sat and made little frocks and tyers for the brothers and sisters.   God knew how every patient needle-thrust was really also a woman's blow for her country.

And now, pale and thin with close, lonely work, the time had come to her at last when it was right to take a respite ; when everybody said it must be ; when Uncle David, just home from Japan, had put his hand in his pocket and pulled out three new fifty-dollar bills, and said to them in his rough way, " There, girls ; take that, and go your lengths." The war was over, and among all the rest here were these two women-soldiers honorably discharged, and resting after the fight.   But nobody at Outledge knew anything of the story.

There is almost always at every summer sojourn some party of persons who are to the rest what the mid-current is to the stream ; who gather to themselves and bear along in their course — in their plans and pleasures and daily doings — the force of all the life of the place.   If any expedition of consequence is afoot, *they* are the expedition ; others may join in, or hold aloof, or be passed by ; in which last cases, it is only in a feeble, rippling fashion that they go their ways and seek some separate pleasure in by-nooks and eddies, while the gay hum of the main channel goes whirling on.   At Outledge, this party was the large and merry school-girl company with Madam Routh.

" I don't see why," said Martha Josselyn, still looking out, as the " little red " left the door of the Green Cottage, — " I don't see why those new girls who came last night should have got into everything in a minute, and

we 've been here a week and don't seem to catch to anything at all. Some people are like burs, I think, or drops
of quicksilver, that always bunch or run together. We
don't *stick*, Susie. What 's the reason ? "

" Some of these young ladies have been at Madam
Routh's ; they were over here last evening. Sin Saxon
knows them very well."

" You knew Effie Saxon at school, too."

" Eight years ago. And this is the little one. That 's
nothing.

" You petted her, and she came to the house. You 've
told her stories hundreds of times. And she sees we 're
all by ourselves."

" She don't see. She does n't think. That 's just the
whole of it."

" People ought to see, then. You would, Sue, and you
know it."

" I 've been used to seeing — and thinking."

" Used ! Yes, indeed ! And she 's been *used* to the
other. Well, it 's queer how the parts are given out.
Shall we go to the pines ? "

A great cliff-side rearing itself up, rough with inacces-
sible crags, bristling with old, ragged pines, and dark
with glooms of close cedars and hemlocks, above a jut-
ting table of rock that reaches out and makes a huge
semicircular base for the mountain, and is in itself a
precipice-pedestal eighty feet sheer up from the river-
bank. Close in against the hill-front, on this platform
of stone, that holds its foot or two of soil, a little, poor,
unshingled house, with a tumble-down picket-fence about

it, attempting the indispensable door-yard of all better
country-dwellings here where the great natural door-yard
or esplanade makes it such an utter nonsense. This is
the place at which the "little red" drew up, ten minutes
later, to leave Prissy Hoskins's parcel.

Dakie Thayne jumped down off the front seat, and helu
up his arms to help Leslie out over the wheel, upon her
declaring that she must go and do the errand herself, to
get a nearer look at Hoskins life.

Dakie Thayne had been asked, at Leslie's suggestion,
to fill the vacant sixth seat beside the driver, the Thoresbys
one and all declining. Mrs. Thoresby was politic : she
would not fall into the wake of this school-girl party at
once. By and by she should be making up her own
excursions, and asking whom she would.

"There's nothing like a boy of that age for use upon a
picnic, Mrs. Linceford," Leslie had pleaded, with playful
parody, in his behalf, when the lady had hinted something
of her former sentiment concerning the encroachments
and monopolies of "boys of that age." And so he came.

The Haddens got Jim Holden to lift them down on the
opposite side, for a run to the verge of the projecting half-
circle of rock that, like a gigantic bay-window or balcony
in the mighty architecture of the hills, looked up and down
the whole perspective of the valley. Jim Holden would
readily have driven them round its very edge upon the
flat, mossy sward, but for Mrs. Linceford's nerves, and
the vague idea of almost an accident having occurred
there lately which pervaded the little party. "Creggin's
horses had backed," as Florrie Arnall said ; and already
the new-comers had picked up, they scarcely knew how,

the incipient tradition, hereafter to grow into an established horror of the " Cliff."

" It was nothing," Jim Holden said ; " only the nigh hoss was a res'less crittur, an' contrived to git his leg over the pole ; no danger with *his* cattle." But Mrs. Linceford cried out in utter remonstrance, and only begged Leslie to be quick, that they might get away from the place altogether.

All this bustle of arrival and discussion and alight-ing had failed, curiously, to turn the head of an odd, un-kempt-looking child, a girl of nine or ten, with an old calico sun-bonnet flung back upon her shoulders, — tangled, sun-burnt hair tossing above it, — gown, innocent of crinoline, clinging to lank, growing limbs, — and bare feet, whose heels were energetically planted at a quite safe distance from each other, to insure a fair base for the centre of gravity, — who, at the moment of their coming, was wrathfully " shoo-ing " off from a bit of rude toy-garden, fenced with ends of twigs stuck upright, a tall Shanghae hen and her one chicken, who had evidently made nothing, morally or physically, of the feeble en-closure.

. " I wish you were dead and in your grav-ies ! " cried the child, achieving, between her righteous indignation and her relenting toward her uncouth pets at the last breath, a sufficiently queer play upon her own word. And with this, the enemy being routed, she turned face to face with Dakie Thayne and Leslie Goldthwaite, coming in at the dilapidated gate.

" They 've scratched up all my four-o'clocks ! " she said. And then her rustic shyness overcame suddenly

all else, and she dragged her great toe back and forth in
the soft mould, and put her forefinger in her mouth, and
looked askance at them from the corners of her eyes.

"Prissy? Prissy Hoskins?" Leslie addressed her in
sweet, inquiring tones. But the child stood still with
finger in mouth, and toe working in the ground, not a bit
harder nor faster, nor changing in the least, for more or
less, the shy look in her face.

"That's your name, is n't it? I 've got something
for you. Won't you come and get it?" Leslie paused,
waiting, — fearing lest a further advance on her own part
might put Prissy altogether to flight. Nothing answered
in the girl's eyes to her words ; there was no lighting up
of desire or curiosity, however restrained ; she stood like
one indifferent or uncomprehending.

"She 's awful deef!" cried a new voice from the doorway. "She ain't that scared. She 's sarcy enough, sometimes."

A woman, middle-aged or more, stood on the rough,
slanting door-stone. She had bare feet, in coarse calf-
skin slippers, stringy petticoats differing only from the
child's in length, sleeves rolled up to the shoulders, no
neck garniture, — not a bit of anything white about her.
Over all looked forth a face sharp and hard, that might
have once been good-looking, in a raw, country fashion,
and that had undoubtedly always been, what it now
was, emphatically Yankee-smart. An inch-wide stripe of
black hair was combed each way over her forehead, and
rolled up on her temples in what, years and years ago,
used to be called most appropriately "flat curls," — these
fastened with long horn sidecombs. Beyond was a strip

of desert, — no hair at all for an inch and a half more toward the crown ; the rest dragged back and tied behind with the relentless tightness that gradually and regularly, by the persistence of years, had accomplished this peculiar belt of clearing. It completed her expression ; it was as a very halo of Yankee saintship crowning the woman who in despite of poverty and every discouragement had always hated, to the very roots of her hair, anything like what she called a " sozzle," — who had always been screwed up and sharp set to hard work. She could n't help the tumble-down fence ; she had no " men-folks " round ; and she could n't have paid for a hundred pickets and a day's carpentering, to have saved her life. She could n't help Prissy's hair even ; for it would kink and curl, and the minute the wind took it " there it was again " ; and it was not time yet, thank goodness ! to harrow it back and begin in her behalf the remarkable engineering which had laid out for herself that broad highway across all the thrifty and energetic bumps up to Veneration, (who knows how much it had had to do with mixing them in one common tingle of mutual and unceasing activity ?) and down again from ear to ear. Inside the poor little house you would find all spick and span ; the old floor white and sanded, the few tins and the pewter spoons shining upon the shelf, the brick hearth and jambs aglow with fresh " redding," table and chairs set back in rectangular tidiness. Only one thing made a litter, or tried to ; a yellow canary that hung in the window and sang "like a house afire," as Aunt Hoskins said, however that is, and flung his seeds about like the old ' Wash at Edmonton," " on both sides of the way."

Prissy was turned out of doors in all pleasant weather; so otherwise the keeping-room stayed trim, and her curly hair grew sunburnt.

"She 's ben deef ever sence she hed the scarlet-fever. Walk in," said the woman, by no means satisfied to let strangers get only the outside impression of her premises, and turning round to lead the way without waiting for a reply. "Come in, Prissy!" she bawled, illustrating her summons with what might be called a beckoning in broad capitals, done with the whole arm from finger-tips to shoulder, twice or thrice.

Leslie followed over the threshold, and Prissy ran by like a squirrel, and perched herself on a stool just under the bird-cage.

"I would n't keep it if 't warn't for her," said Aunt Hoskins, apologetically. She was Prissy's aunt, holding no other close domestic relation to living thing, and so had come to be "Aunt Hoskins" in the whole region round about, so far as she was known at all. "It 's the only bird she can hear sing of a morning. It 's as good as all out-doors to her, and I haint the heart to make her do without it. *I* 've done without most things, but it don't appear to me as if I *could* do without them. Take a seat, do."

"I thank you, but my friends are waiting. I 've brought something for Prissy, from Miss Craydocke at the hotel." And Leslie held out the package which Dakie Thayne, waiting at the door, had put into her hand as she came in.

"Lawful suz! Prissy! if 't ain't another book!" cried the good woman, as Prissy, quick to divine the meaning

of the parcel, the like of which she had been made accus-
tomed to before, sprang to her aunt's side within hearing
of her exclamation. "If she ain't jest the feelingest and
thoughtfullest— Well! open it yourself, child; there's
no good of a bundle if you don't."

Poor Prissy was thus far happy that she had not been
left in the providence of her little life to utter ignorance
of this greatest possible delight — a common one to more
outwardly favored children — of a real parcel all one's own.
The book, without the brown paper and string, would have
been as nothing, comparatively.

Leslie could not but linger to see it untied. There came
out a book, — a wonderful big book, — Grimm's Tales; and
some little papers fell to the floor. These were flower-
seeds, — bags labelled "Petunia," "Candytuft," "Double
Balsam," "Portulaca."

"Why, Prissy!" shouted Miss Hoskins in her ear as
she picked them up, and read the names; "them's elegant things! They'll beat your four-o'clocks all to
nothin'. It's lucky the old Shank-high did make a
clearin' of 'em. Tell Miss Craydocke," she continued,
turning again to Leslie, "that I'm comin' down myself,
to — no, I *can't* thank her! She's made a *life* for that
air child, out o' nothin', a'most!"

Leslie stood hushed and penetrated in the presence of
this good deed, and the joy and gratitude born of it.

"This ain't all, you see; nor 't ain't nothin' new.
She's ben at it these two year; learnin' the child to
read, an' tellin' her things, an' settin' her to hunt 'em
out, and to do for herself. She was crazy about flowers,
allers, an' stories; but, lor, I couldn't stop to tell 'em to

her, an' I never knew but one or two; an' now she can read 'em off to me, like a minister. She's told her a lot o' stuff about the rocks, — *I* can't make head nor tail on 't; but it 'ud please you to see her fetchin' 'em in by the apern-full, an' goin'·on about 'em, that is, if there was reely any place to put 'em afterwards. That's the wust on 't. I tell you, it *is* jest *makin'* a life out o' pieces that come to hand. Here's the girl, an' there's the woods an' rocks; there's all there was to do with, or likely to be; but she found the gumption an' the willingness, an' she's done it!"

Prissy came close over to Leslie with her book in her hand. "Wait a minute," she said, with the effort in her tone peculiar to the deaf. "I've got something to send back."

"*If* it's convenient, you mean,' put in Aunt Hoskins, sharply. "She's as blunt as a broomstick — that child is."

But Prissy had sprung away in her squirrel-like fashion, and now came back, bringing with her something really to make one's eyes water, if one happened, at least, to be ever so little of a geologist, — a mass of quartz rock as large as she could grasp with her two hands, shot through at three different angles with three long, superb, columnar crystals of clear, pale-green beryl. If Professor Dana had known this exact locality, and a more definite name for the "Cliff," would n't he have had it down in his Supplement with half a dozen exclamation-points after the "beryl"!

"I found it a-purpose!" said Prissy, with the utmost simplicity, putting the heavy specimen out of her own

nands into Leslie's. "She's been a-wantin' it this great
while, and we've looked for it everywheres!"

"A-purpose" it did seem as if the magnificent fragment had been laid in the way of the child's zealous and
grateful search. "There were only the rocks," as Aunt
Hoskins said ; in no other way could she so joyously have
acknowledged the kindness that had brightened now three
summers of her life.

"It'll bother you, I'm afeard," said the woman.

"No, indeed! I shall *like* to take it for you," continued
Leslie, with a warm earnestness, stooping down to the little girl, and speaking in her clear, glad tone close to her
cheek. "I only wish *I* could find something to take her
myself." And with that, close to the little red-brown
cheek as she was, she put the period of a quick kiss to
her words.

"Come again, and we'll hunt for some together," said
the child, with instant response of cordiality.

"I will come — if I possibly can," was Leslie's last
word, and then she and Dakie Thayne hurried back to
the wagon.

The Haddens had just got in again upon their side.
They were full of exclamations about the wonderful view
up and down the long valley-reaches.

"You need n't tell *me!*" cried Elinor, in high enthusiasm. "I don't care a bit for the geography of it.
That great aisle goes straight from Lake Umbagog to
the Sound!"

"It is a glorious picture," said Mrs. Linceford. "But
I've had a little one, that you've lost. You've no idea,
Leslie, what a lovely tableau you have been making, —

you and Dakie, with that old woman and the blowsy child ! "

Leslie blushed.

" You 'll never look prettier, if you try ever so hard."

" Don't, Mrs. Linceford ! "

" Why not ? " said Jeannie. " It 's only a pity, I think, that you could n't have known it at the time. They say we don't know when we 're happiest ; and we *can't* know when we 're prettiest ; so where 's the satisfaction ? "

" That 's part of your mistake, Jeannie, perhaps," returned her sister. " If you had been there you 'd have spoiled the picture."

" Look at that ! " exclaimed Leslie, showing her beryl. " That 's for Miss Craydocke." And then, when the first utterances of amazement and admiration were over, she told them the story of the child, and her misfortune, and of what Miss Craydocke had done. " *That 's* beautiful, I think," said she. " And it 's the sort of beauty, may be, that one might feel as one went along. I wish I could find — a diamond — for that woman ! "

" Thir garnits on Feather-Cap," put in Jim the driver.

" O, *will* you show us where ? "

" Well, 't ain't nowhers in partickler," replied Jim. " It 's jest as you light on 'em. And you would n't know the best ones when you did. I 've seen 'em, — dead, dull-lookin' round stones that 'll crack open chock full o' red garnits, as an egg is o' meat."

" Geodes ! " cried Dakie Thayne.

Jim Holden turned round and looked at him as if he thought he had got hold of some new-fashioned expletive, — possibly a pretty hard one.

They came down, now, on the other side of the Cliff, and struck the ford. This diverted and absorbed their thoughts, for none of the ladies had ever forded a river before.

"Are you sure it's safe?" asked Mrs. Linceford.

"Safe as meetin'," returned Jim. "I'd drive across with my eyes shot."

"O, don't!" cried Elinor.

"I ain't agoin' ter; but I could, — an' the hosses too, for that matter."

It was exciting, nevertheless, when the water in mid-channel came up nearly to the body of the wagon, and the swift ripples deluded the eye into almost conviction that horses, vehicle, and all were gaining not an inch in forward progress, but drifting surely down. They came up out of the depths, however, with a tug, and a swash, and a drip all over, and a scrambling of hoofs on the pebbles, at the very point aimed at in such apparently sidelong fashion, — the wheel-track that led them up the bank and into the ten-mile pine-woods through which they were to skirt the base of the Cairn and reach Feather-Cap on his accessible side. It was one long fragrance and stillness and shadow.

They overtook the Routh party at the beginning of the mountain-path. The pine-woods stretched on over the gradual slope, as far as they would climb before dinner. Otherwise the midday heats would have been too much for them. This was the easy part of the way, and there was breath for chat and merriment.

Just within the upper edge of the woods, in a comparatively smooth opening, they halted. Here they spread their picnic; while up above, on the bare, open rock, the young men kindled their fire, and heated the coffee; and here they ate and drank, and rested through the noontide.

Light clouds flitted between the mountains and the heavens, later in the day, and flung bewildering, dreamy shadows on the far-off steeps, and dropped a gracious veil over the bald forehead and sun-bleak shoulders of Feather-Cap. It was "weather just made for them," as fortunate excursionists are wont to say.

Sin Saxon was all life, and spring, and fun. She climbed at least three Feather-Caps, dancing from stone to stone with tireless feet, and bounding back and forth with every gay word that it occurred to her to say to anybody. Pictures? She made them incessantly. She was a living dissolving view. You no sooner got one bright look or graceful attitude than it was straightway shifted into another. She kept Frank Scherman at her side for the first half-hour, and then, perhaps, his admiration or his muscles tired, for he fell back a little to help Madam Routh up a sudden ridge, and afterwards, somehow, merged himself in the quieter group of strangers.

By and by one of the Arnalls whispered to Mattie Shannon. "He's sidled off with her, at last. Did you ever know such a fellow for a new face? But it's partly the petticoat. He's such an artist's eye for color. He was raving about her all the while she stood hanging those shawls among the pines to keep the wind from Mrs. Linceford. She is n't downright pretty either. But she's got up *exquisitely*!"

Leslie Goldthwaite, in her lovely mountain-dress, her

bright bloom from enjoyment and exercise, with the
stray light through the pines burnishing the bronze of
her hair, had innocently made a second picture, it would
seem.   One such effects deeper.impression, sometimes,
than the confusing splendor of incessant changes.

"Are you looking for something?   Can I help you?"
Frank Scherman had said, coming up to her, as she and
her friend Dakie, a little apart from the others, were
poking among some loose pebbles.

"Nothing that I have lost," Leslie answered, smiling.
"Something I have a very presumptuous wish to find.
A splendid garnet geode, if you please!"

"That's not at all impossible," returned the young
man.   "We'll have it before we go down, — see if we
don't!"   .

Frank Scherman knew a good deal about Feather-Cap,
and something of geologizing.   So he and Leslie — Dakie Thayne, in his unswerving devotion, still accompany-
ing — "sidled off" together, took a long turn round
under the crest, talking very pleasantly — and restfully,
after Sin Saxon's continuous brilliancy — all the way.
How they searched among loose drift under the cliff, —
how Mr. Scherman improvised a hammer from a slice of
rock, — and how, after many imperfect specimens, they
did at last "find a-purpose" an irregular oval of dull,
dusky stone, which burst with a stroke into two chalices
of incrusted crimson crystals, — I ought to be too near
the end of a long chapter to tell.   But this search, and
this finding, and the motive of it, were the soul and the
crown of Leslie's pleasure for the day.   She did not even
stop to think how long she had had Frank Scherman's

attention all to herself, or the triumph that it was in the
eyes of the older girls, among whom he was excessively
admired, and not very disguisedly competed for. She
did not know how fast she was growing to be a sort of
admiration herself among them, in their girls' fashion, or
what she might do, if she chose, in the way of small,
early belleship here at Outledge with such beginning, —
how she was " getting on," in short, as girls express it.
And so, as Jeannie Hadden asked, " Where was the satisfaction ? "

" You never knew anything like it," said Jeannie to
her friend Ginevra, talking it all over with her that evening in a bit of a visit to Mrs. Thoresby's room. " I never
saw anybody take so among strangers. Madam Routh
was delighted with her ; and so, I should think, was Mr.
Scherman. They say he hates trouble ; but he took her
all round the top of the mountain, hammering stones for
her to find a geode."

" That 's the newest dodge," said Mrs. Thoresby, with
a little sarcastic laugh. " Girls of that sort are always
looking for geodes." After this, Mrs. Thoresby had
always a little well-bred venom for Leslie Goldthwaite.

At the same time, Leslie herself, coming out on the
piazza for a moment after tea, met Miss Craydocke approaching over the lawn. She had only her errand to
introduce her, but she would not lose the opportunity.
She went straight up to the little woman, in a frank,
sweet way. But a bit of embarrassment underneath, the
real respect that made her timid, perhaps a little nervous
fatigue after the excitement and exertion of the day, did
what nerves and embarrassment, and reverence itself,

will do sometimes, — played a trick with her perfectly clear thought on its way to her tongue.

"Miss Graywacke, I believe?" she said, and instantly knew the dreadful thing that she had done.

"Exactly," said the lady, with an amused little smile.

"O, I *do* beg your pardon," began Leslie, blushing all over.

"No need, — no need. Do you think I don't know what name I go by, behind my back? They suppose because I 'm old and plain and single, and wear a front, and don't understand rats and the German, that I 'm deaf and blind and stupid. But I believe I get as much as they do out of their jokes, after all." The dear old soul took Leslie by both her hands as she spoke, and looked a whole world of gentle benignity at her out of two soft gray eyes, and then she laughed again. This woman had no *self* to be hurt.

"We stopped at the Cliff this morning," Leslie took heart to say; "and they were *so* glad of your parcel, — the little girl and her aunt. And Prissy gave me something to bring back to you, — a splendid specimen of beryl that she has found."

"Then my mind 's at rest!" said Miss Craydocke, cheerier than ever. "I was sure she 'd break her neck, or pull the mountain down on her head some day looking for it."

"Would you like — I 've found — I should like you to have that too, — a garnet geode from Feather-Cap?" Leslie thought she had done it very clumsily, and in a hurry, after all.

"Will you come over to my little room, dear, — number fifteen, in the west wing, — to-morrow some time, with your stones? I want to see more of you."

There was a deliberate, gentle emphasis upon her words. If the grandest person of whom she had ever known had said to Leslie Goldthwaite, " I want to see more of you," she would not have heard it with a warmer thrill than she felt that moment a: her heart.

VIII.

IT was a glorious July morning, and there was nothing particular on foot.   In the afternoon, there would be drives and walks, perhaps; for some hours, now, there would be intensifying heat.   The sun had burned away every cloud that had hung rosy about his rising, and the great gray flanks of Washington glared in a pale scorch close up under the sky, whose blue fainted in the flooding presence of the full white light of such unblunted day. Here and there, adown his sides, something flashed out in a clear, intense dazzle, like an enormous crystal cropping from the granite, and blazing with reflected splendor.   These were the leaps of water from out dark rifts into the sun.

"Everybody will be in the pines to-day," said Martha Josselyn.   "I think it is better when they all go off and leave us."

"We can go up under our rock," said Sue, putting stockings and mending cotton into a large, light basket. "Have you got the chess-board?   What *should* we do without our mending-day?"

These two girls had bought new stockings for all the little feet at home, that the weekly darning might be less for the mother while they were away; and had come with their own patiently-cared-for old hose, "which they should have nothing else to do but to embroider."

They had made a sort of holiday, in their fashion, of mending-day at home, till it had come to seem like a pos-

:itive treat and rest; and the habit was so strong upon
them that they hailed it even here. They always got out
their little chess-board, when they sat down to the big
basket together. They could darn, and consider, and
move, and darn again ; and so could keep it up all day
long, as else even they would have found it nearly intolerable to do. So, though they seemed slower at it, they
really in the end saved time. Thursday night saw the
tedious work all done, and the basket piled with neatly
folded pairs, like a heap of fine white rolls. This was a
great thing, and " enough for one day," as Mrs. Josselyn
said. It was disastrous if they once began to lie over.
If they could be disposed of between sun and sun, the
girls were welcome to any play they could get out of it.

    " There they go, those two together. Always to the
pines, and always with a work-basket," said Leslie Goldthwaite, sitting on the piazza step at the Green Cottage,
by Mrs. Linceford's feet, the latter lady occupying a
Shaker rocking-chair behind. " What nice girls they
seem to be, — and nobody appears to know them much,
beyond a ' good morning ! ' "

    " Henny-penny, Goosie-poosie, Turkey-lurky, Ducky-
daddles, *and* Chicken Little ! " said Mrs. Linceford,
counting up from thumb to little finger. " Dakie Thayne
and Miss Craydocke, Marmaduke Wharne and these
two, — they just make it out," she continued, counting
back again. " Whatever you do, Les, don't make up to
Fox Lox at last, for all our sakes ! "

    Out came Dakie Thayne, at this point, upon them,
with his hands full. " Miss Leslie, *could* you head these
needles for me with black wax ? I want them for my

butterflies, and I 've made *such* a daub and scald of it! I 've blistered three fingers, and put lop-sided heads to two miserable pins, and left no end of wax splutters on my table. I have n't but two sticks more, and the deacon don't keep any ; I must try to get a dozen pins out of it, at least." He had his sealing-wax and a lighted " homespun candle," as Leslie called the dips of Mrs. Green's manufacture, in one hand, and a pincushion stuck full of needles waiting for tops, in the other.

" I told you so," said Mrs. Linceford to Leslie. " That 's it, then ? " she asked of Dakie Thayne.

" What, ma'am ? "

" Butterflies. I knew you 'd some hobby or other, — I said so. I 'm glad it 's no worse," she answered, in her pleasant, smiling way. Dakie Thayne had a great liking for Mrs. Linceford, but he adored Leslie Goldthwaite.

" I 'd like to show them to you, if you 'd care," he said. " I 've got some splendid ones. One great Turnus, that I brought with me in the chrysalis, that hatched out while I was at Jefferson. I rolled it up in a paper for the journey, and fastened it in the crown of my hat. I 've had it ever since last fall. The asterias worms are spinning now, — the early ones. They 're out on the carrot-tops in shoals. I 'm feeding up a dozen of 'em in a box. They 're very handsome, — bright green with black and yellow spots, — and it 's the queerest thing to see them stiffen out and change."

" *Can* you ? Do they do it all at once ? " asked Etty Thoresby, slipping into the rocking-chair, as Mrs. Linceford, by whom she had come and placed herself within the last minute, rose and went in to follow her laundress, just then going up the stairs with her basket.

"Pretty much. It seems so. The first thing you know they stick themselves up by their tails, and spin a noose to hang back their heads in, and there they are, like a pappoose in a basket. Then their skin turns a queer, dead, ashy color, and grows somehow straight and tight, and they only squirm a little in a feeble way now and then, and grow stiffer and stiffer, till they can't squirm at all, and then they 're mummies, and that 's the end of it till the butterflies are born. It 's a strange thing to see a live creature go into its own shroud, and hang itself up to turn into a corpse. Sometimes a live one, crawling round to find a place for itself, will touch a mummy accidentally; and then, when they 're not quite gone, I 've seen 'em give an odd little quiver, under the shell, as if they were almost at peace, and did n't want to be intruded on, or called back to earthly things, and the new-comer takes the hint, and respects privacy, and moves himself off to find quarters somewhere else. Miss Leslie, how splendidly you 're doing those! What 's the difference, I wonder, between girls' fingers and boys'? I could n't make those atoms of balls so round and perfect, 'if I died and suffered,' as Miss Hoskins says."

"It 's only centrifugal force," said Leslie, spinning round between her finger and thumb a needle to whose head she had just touched a globule of the bright black wax. "The world and a pin-head, — both made on the same principle."

The Haddens and Imogen Thoresby strolled along together, and added themselves to the group.

"Let's go over to the hotel, Leslie. We've seen nothing of the girls since just after breakfast. They must be up in the hall, arranging about the tableaux."

"I'll come by and by, if you want me; don't wait. I'm going to finish these — properly"; and she dipped and twirled another needle with dainty precision, in the pause between her words.

"Have you got a lot of brothers at home, Miss Leslie?" asked Dakie Thayne.

"Two," replied Leslie. "Not at home, though, now. One at Exeter, and the other at Cambridge. Why?"

"I was thinking it would be bad — what do you call it — political economy or something, if you had n't any, that's all."

"Mamma wants you," said Ginevra Thoresby, looking out at the door to call her sisters. "She's in the Haughtleys' room. They're talking about the wagon for Minster Rock to-night. What *do* you take up your time with that boy for?" she added, not inaudibly, as she and Imogen turned away together.

"O dear!" cried blunt Etty, lingering, "I wonder if she meant me. I want to hear about the caterpillars. Mamma thinks the Haughtleys are such nice people, because they came in their own carriage, and they've got such big trunks, and a saddle-horse, and elegant dressing-cases, and ivory-backed brushes! I wish she did n't care so about such things."

Mrs. Thoresby would have been shocked to hear her little daughter's arrangement and version of her ideas. She had simply been kind to these strangers on their arrival — in their own comfortable carriage — a few days since; had stepped forward, — as somehow it seemed to devolve upon her, with her dignified air and handsome gray curls, when she chose, to do, — representing by a kind of tacit consent the household in general, as somebody in every such sojourn usually will; had interested herself about their rooms, which were near her own, and had reported of them, privately, among other things noted in these first glimpses, that "they had everything about them in the most *perfect* style; ivory-backed brushes, and lovely inlaid dressing-cases, Ginevra; the best all *through*, and no sham!" Yes indeed, if that could but be said truly, and need not stop at brushes and boxes!

Imogen came back presently, and called to Etty from the stairs, and she was obliged to go. Jeannie Hadden waited till they were fairly off the landing, and then walked away herself, saying nothing, but wearing a slightly displeased air.

Mrs. Thoresby and her elder daughter had taken a sort of dislike to Dakie Thayne. They seemed to think he wanted putting down. Nobody knew anything about him; he was well enough in his place, perhaps; but why should he join himself to their party? The Routh girls had Frank Scherman, and two or three other older attendants; among them he was simply not thought of, often, at all. If it had not been for Leslie and Mrs. Linceford, he would have found himself in Outledge, what boys of his age are apt to find themselves in the world at large, — a sort of odd or stray, not provided for anywhere in the general scheme of society. For this very reason, discerning it quickly, Leslie had been loyal to him; and he, with all his boy-vehemence of ad-

miration and devotion, was loyal to her. She had the feeling, motherly and sisterly in its mingled instinct, by which
all true and fine feminine natures are moved, in behalf
of the man-nature in its dawn, that so needs sympathy
and gentle consideration and provision, and that certain
respect which calls forth and fosters self-respect ; — to bo
allowed and acknowledged to be somebody, lest for the
want of this it should fail, unhappily, ever to be anybody.
She was not aware of it; she only followed her kindly
instinct. So she was doing, unconsciously, one of the best
early bits of her woman-work in the world.

Once in a while it occurred to Leslie Goldthwaite to
wonder why it was that she was able to forget — that she
found she had forgotten, in a measure — those little self-
absorptions that she had been afraid of, and that had puzzled her in her thoughtful moments. She was glad to
be " taken up " with something that could please Dakie
Thayne, or to go over to the Cliff and see Prissy Hoskins,
and tell her a story, or help Dakie to fence in safely her
beds of flower-seedlings, (she had not let her first visit be
her last, in these weeks since her introduction there,) or
to sit an hour with dear old Miss Craydocke and help her
in a bit of charity work, and hear her sweet, simple, genial
talk. She had taken up her little opportunities as they
came, — was it by instinct only, or through a tender
Spirit-leading, that she winnowed them and chose the
best, and had been kept so a little out of the drift and
hurry that might else have frothed away the hours ?
" Give us our daily bread," " Lead us not into temptation," — they have to do with each other, if we " know
the daily bread when we see it." But that also is of the
grace of God.

There was the beginning of fruit under the leaf with Leslie Goldthwaite ; and the fine life-current was setting itself that way with its best impulse and its rarest particles.

The pincushion was well filled with the delicate, bristling, tiny-headed needles, when Miss Craydocke appeared, walking across, under her great brown sun-umbrella, from the hotel.

"If you 've nothing else to do, my dears, suppose we go over to the pines together? Where 's Miss Jeannie? Would n't she like it? All the breeze there is haunts them always."

"I 'm always ready for the pines," said Leslie. "Here, Dakie, I hope you 'll catch a butterfly for every pin. O, now I think of it, have you found your *elephant?* "

"Yes, half-way up the garret-stairs. I can't feed him comfortably, Miss Leslie. He wants to eat incessantly, and the elm-leaves wilt so quickly, if I bring them in, that the first thing I know, he 's out of proper provender and off on a raid. He needs to be on the tree ; but then I should lose him."

Leslie thought a minute. "You might tie up a branch with mosquito-netting," she said.

"Is n't that bright? I 'll go right and do it, — only I have n't any netting," said he.

"Mrs. Linceford has. I 'll go and beg a piece for you. And then — if you 'll just sit here a minute — I 'll come, Miss Craydocke."

When she came back, she brought Jeannie with her. To use a vulgar proverb, Jeannie's nose was rather out

of joint since the Haughtleys had arrived. Ginevra
Thoresby was quite engrossed with them, and this often
involved Imogen.   There was only room for six in Captain Green's wagon, and nothing had been said to Jeannie
about the drive to Minster Rock.

Leslie had hanging upon her finger, also, the finest and
whitest and most graceful of all possible little splint baskets, only just big enough to carry a bit of such work as
was in it now, — a strip of sheer, delicate grass-linen,
which needle and thread, with her deft guidance, were
turning into a cobweb border, by a weaving of lace-lines,
strong, yet light, where the woof of the original material
had been drawn out.   It was "done for odd-minute
work, and was better than anything she could buy."
Prettier it certainly was, when, with a finishing of the
merest edge of lace, it came to encircle her round, fair
arms and shoulders, or to peep out with its dainty revela-
tion among the gathering treasures of the linen-drawer I
told you of.   She had accomplished yards of it already for
her holiday-work.

She had brought the netting, as she promised, for
Dakie Thayne, who received it with thanks, and straightway hastened off to get his "elephant" and a piece of
string, and to find a convenient elm-branch which he
could convert into a cage-pasture.

"I 'll come round to the pines afterward," he said.

And, just then, Sin Saxon's bright face and pretty figure showing themselves on the hotel piazza, with a seeking look and gesture, Jeannie and Elinor were drawn off
also to ask about the tableaux, and see if they were
wanted, with the like promise that "they would come

presently." So Miss Craydocke and Leslie walked slowly round, under the sun-umbrella, to the head of the ledge, by themselves.

Up this rocky promontory it was very pretty little climbing, over the irregular turf-covered crags that made the ascent; and once up, it was charming. A natural grove of stately old pine-trees, with their glory of tasselled foliage and their breath of perfume, crowned and sheltered it; and here had been placed at cosey angles, under the deepest shade, long, broad, elastic benches of boards, sprung from rock to rock, and made secure to stakes, or held in place by convenient irregularities of the rock itself. Pine-trunks and granite offered rough support to backs that could so fit themselves; and visitors found out their favorite seats, and spent hours there, with books or work, or looking forth in a luxurious listlessness from out the cool upon the warm, bright valley-picture, and the shining water wandering down from far heights and unknown solitudes to see the world.

" It 's better so," said Miss Craydocke, when the others left them. "I had a word I wanted to say to you. What do you suppose those two came up here to the mountains for ? " And Miss Craydocke nodded up, indicatively, toward the two girl-figures just visible by their draperies in a nook of rock beyond and above the benches.

" To get the good of them — as we did — I suppose," Leslie answered, wondering a little what Miss Craydocke might exactly mean.

" I suppose so, too," was the reply. " And I suppose — the Lord's love came with them ! I suppose He cares

whether they get the full of the good. And yet I think
He leaves it, like everything else, a little to us."

Leslie's heart beat quicker, hearing these words. It
beat quicker always when such thoughts were touched.
She was shy of seeking them; she almost tried, in an
involuntary way, to escape them at first, when they were
openly broached; yet she longed always, at the same
time, for a deeper understanding of them. "I should
like to know the Miss Josselyns better," she said, presently, when Miss Craydocke made no haste to speak
again. "I have been thinking so this morning. I have
thought so very often. But they seem so quiet, always.
One does n't like to intrude."

"They ought to be more with young people," Miss
Craydocke went on. "And they ought to do less rip-
ping and sewing and darning, if it could be managed.
They brought three trunks with them. And what do
you think the third is full of?"

Leslie had no idea, of course.

"Old winter dresses. To be made over. For the
children at home. So that their mother may be coaxed
to take her turn and go away upon a visit when they get
back, seeing that the fall sewing will be half done!
That 's a pretty coming to the mountains for two tired-
out young things, I think!"

"O dear!" cried Leslie, pitifully; and then a secret
compunction seized her, thinking of her own little elegant,
odd-minute work, which was all she had to interfere with
mountain-pleasure.

"And is n't it some of our business, if we could get at
it?" asked Miss Craydocke, concluding.

"Dear Miss Craydocke!" said Leslie, with a warm brightness in her face, as she looked up, "the world is full of business; but so few people find out any but their own! Nobody but you dreamt of this, or of Prissy Hoskins, till you showed us, — or of all the little Wigleys. How do you come to know, when other people go on in their own way, and see nothing, — like the priests and Levites?" This last she added by a sudden occurrence and application, that half answered, beforehand, her own question.

"When we think of people's needs as the *Master's!*" said Miss Craydocke, evading herself, and never minding her syntax. "When we think what every separate soul is to him, that he came into the world to care for as God cares for the sparrows! It's my faith that he's never gone away from his work, dear; that his love lies alongside every life, and in all its experience; and that his life is in his love; and that if we want to find him — *there* we may! 'Inasmuch as ye have done it unto the least of these, ye have done it unto me.'" She grew eloquent — the plain, simple-speaking woman — when something that was great and living to her would find utterance.

"How do you mean that?" said Leslie, with a sort of abruptness, as of one who must have definiteness, but who hurried with her asking, lest after a minute she might not dare. "That He really knows, and thinks, of every special thing and person, — and cares? Or only *would?*"

"I take it as He said it," said Miss Craydocke. "'All power is given me in heaven and in earth.' 'And lo! I

am with you always, even unto the end of the world!'
He put the two together himself, dear!"

A great, warm, instant glow seemed to rush over Leslie
inwardly. In the light and quickening of it, other words
shone out and declared themselves. "Abide in me, and
I in you. As the branch cannot bear fruit of itself, except it abide in the vine, no more can ye, except ye
abide in me." And this was the abiding! The sympathy, the interest, that found itself side by side with
His! The faith that felt His uniting presence with all!

To this child of sixteen came a moment's glimpse of
what might be, truly, that life which is "hid with Christ
in God," and which has its blessed work with the Lord
in the world; — came, with the word of a plain, old, un-
considered woman, whom heedless girls made daily sport
of; — came, bringing with it "old and new," like a
householder of the kingdom of heaven; showing how the
life and the fruit are inextricably one, — how the growth
and the withering are inevitably determined!

They reached the benches now; they saw the Josselyns busy up beyond, with their chess-board between
them, and their mending-basket at their feet; they would
not go now and interrupt their game.

The seat which the sisters had chosen, because it was
just a quiet little corner for two, was a nook scooped out,
as it were, in a jut of granite; hollowed in behind and
perpendicularly to a height above their heads, and em-
bracing a mossy little flat below, so that it seemed like a
great solid arm-chair into which two could get together,
and a third could not possibly intrude.

Miss Craydocke and Leslie settled themselves, and both

were silent. Presently Leslie spoke again, giving out a
fragmentary link of the train of thought that had been
going on in her. "If it were n't for just one thing!"
she said, and there she stopped.

"What?" asked Miss Craydocke, as not a bit at a loss
to make out the unseen connection.

"The old puzzle. We *have* to think and work a
good deal of the time for ourselves. And then we lose
sight —"

"Of Him? Why?"

Leslie said no more, but waited. Miss Craydocke's
tone was clear, untroubled. The young girl looked,
therefore, for this clear confidence to be spoken out.

"Why? since He is close to *our* life also, and cares
tenderly for that? — since, if we let him possess himself
of it, it is one of his own channels, by which he still
gives himself unto the world? He did n't do it all in one
single history of three years, my child, or thirty-three,
out there in Judæa. He keeps on — so I believe —
through every possible way and circumstance of human
living now, if only the life is grafted on his. The Vine
and the branches, and God tending all. And the fruit is
the kingdom of heaven."

It is never too late, and never impossible, for a human
face to look beautiful. In the soft light and shadow of the
stirring pines, with the moving from within of that which
at once illumined and veiled, with an exultation and an
awe, there came a glory over the homely and faded features which they could neither bar nor dim. And the
thought took possession of the word and tone, and made
them simply grand and heavenly musical.

After that they sat still again,—it matters not how many minutes. The crisp green spines rustled dreamily over their heads; the wild birds called to each other, far back in the closer lying woods; the water glanced on, millions of new drops every instant making the selfsame circles and gushes and falls, and the wealth of summer sunshine holding and vivifying all. Leslie had word and scene stamped together on her spirit and memory in those moments. There was a Presence in the hush and beauty. Two souls were here met together in the name of the living Christ. And for that there is the promise.

Martha Josselyn and her sister sat and played and mended on.

By and by Dakie Thayne came; said a bright word or two; glanced round, in restless boy-fashion, as if taking in the elements of the situation, and considering what was to be made out of it; perceived the pair at chess; and presently, with his mountain stick, went springing away from point to point, up and around the piles and masses of rock and mound that made up the broadening ascent of the ledge.

"Check to your queen," said Sue.

Martha put her elbow up on her knee, and held her needle suspended by its thread. Sue darned away, and got a great hole laid lengthwise with smooth lines, before her threatening move had been provided for. Then a red knight came with gallant leap, right down in the midst of the white forces, menacing in his turn right and left; and Martha drew a long sigh, and sat back, and poised her needle-lance again, and went to work; and it was Sue's turn to lean over the board with knit brows and holden breath.

Something peered over the rock above them at this moment. A boy's head, from which the cap had been removed.

"If only they 'll play now, and not chatter!" thought Dakie Thayne, lying prone along the cliff above, and putting up his elbows to rest his head between his hands. "This 'll be jolly, if it don't turn to eavesdropping. Poor old Noll! I have n't had a game since I played with him!"

Sue would not withdraw her attack. She planted a bishop so that, if the knight should move, it would open a course straight down toward a weak point beside the red king.

"She means to 'fight it out on that line, if it takes all summer,'" Dakie went on within himself, having grasped, during the long pause before Sue's move, the whole position. "They 're no fools at it, to have got it into a shape like that! I 'd just like Noll to see it!"

Martha looked, and drew a thread or two into her stocking, and looked again. Then she stabbed her cotton-ball with her needle, and put up both hands — one with the white stocking-foot still drawn over it — beside her temples. At last she castled.

Sue was as calm as the morning. She always grew calm and strong as the game drew near the end. She had even let her thoughts go off to other things while Martha pondered and she wove in the cross-threads of her darn.

"I wonder, Martha," she said now, suddenly, before attending to the new aspect of the board, "if I could n't do without that muslin skirt I made to wear under my

piña, and turn it into a couple of white waists to carry
home to mother? If she goes away, you know — "

" Aigh ! "

It was a short, sharp, unspellable sound that came from
above. Sue started, and a red piece rolled from the board.
Then there was a rustling and a crashing and a leaping,
and by a much shorter and more hazardous way than he
had climbed, Dakie Thayne came down and stood before
them. "I had to let you know! I could n't listen. I
was in hopes you would n't talk. Don't move, please!
I 'll find the man. I do beg your pardon, — I had no
business, — but I so like chess, — when it 's any sort of
a game ! "

While he spoke, he was looking about the base of the
rock, and by good fortune spied and pounced upon the bit
of bright-colored ivory, which had rolled and rested itself
against a hummock of sod.

" May I see it out ? " he begged, approaching, and putting the piece upon the board. "You must have played
a good deal," looking at Sue.

" We play often at home, my sister and I; and I had
some good practice in — " There she stopped.

" In the hospital," said Martha, with the sharp little
way she took up sometimes. " Why should n't you tell
of it ? "

" Has Miss Josselyn been in the hospitals?" asked Dakie
Thayne, with a certain quick change in his tone.

" For the best of two years," Martha answered.

At this moment, seeing how Dakie was breaking the
ice for them, up came Miss Craydocke and Leslie Goldthwaite.

"Miss Leslie! Miss Craydocke! This lady has been away among our soldiers — in the hospitals — half through the war! Perhaps — did you ever — " But with that he broke off. There was a great flush on his face, and his eyes glowed with boy-enthusiasm lit at the thought of the war, and of brave men, and of noble, ministering women, of whom he suddenly found himself face to face with one.

The game of chess got swept together. "It was as good as over," Martha Josselyn said. And these five sat down together among the rocks, and in half an hour, after weeks of mere "good-mornings" they had grown to be old friends. But Dakie Thayne — he best knew why — left his fragment of a question unfinished.

IX.

THE "by-and-by" people came at last, — Jeannie, and Elinor, and Sin Saxon, and the Arnalls, and Josie Scherman. They wanted Leslie, — to tell and ask her half a hundred things about the projected tableaux. If it had only been Miss Craydocke and the Josselyns sitting together, with Dakie Thayne, how would that have concerned them, — the later comers? It would only have been a bit of "the pines" preoccupied : they would have found a place for themselves, and gone on with their own chatter. But Leslie's presence made all the difference. The little group became the nucleus of the enlarging circle. Miss Craydocke had known very well how this would be.

They asked this and that of Leslie which they had come to ask ; and she would keep turning to the Josselyns and appealing to them ; so they were drawn in. There was a curtain to be made, first of all. Miss Craydocke would undertake that, drafting Leslie and the Miss Josselyns to help her ; they should all come to her room early to-morrow, and they would have it ready by ten o'clock. Leslie wondered a little that she found *work* for them to do : a part of the play she thought would have been better ; but Miss Craydocke knew how that must come about. Besides, she had more than one little line to lay and to pull, this serpent-wise old maiden, in behalf of her ultimate designs concerning them.

I can't stay here under the pines and tell you all their

7

talk this summer morning, — how Sin Saxon grew social
and saucy with the quiet Miss Josselyns; how she fell
upon the mending-basket and their notability, and declared that the most foolish and pernicious proverb in the
world was that old thing about a stitch in time saving
nine; it might save certain special stitches; but how
about the *time* itself, and *other* stitches? She did n't
believe in it, — running round after a darning-needle and
forty other things, the minute a thread broke, and dropping whatever else one had in hand, to let it ravel itself
all out again; "she believed in a good big basket, in a
dark closet, and laying up there for a rainy day, and being
at peace in the pleasant weather. Then, too, there was
another thing; she did n't believe in notability itself, at
all: the more one was fool enough to know, the more
one had to do, all one's life long. Providence always
took care of the lame and the lazy; and, besides, those
capable people never had contented minds. They
could n't keep servants: their own fingers were always
itching to do things better. Her sister Effie was a lam-
entable instance. She 'd married a man, — well, not
very rich, — and she had set out to learn and direct everything. The consequence was, she was like Eve after the
apple, — she knew good and evil; and was n't the garden
just a wilderness after that? She never thought of it
before, but she believed that was exactly what that old
poem in Genesis was written for!"

How Miss Craydocke answered, with her gentle, toler-
ant common-sense, and right thought, and wide-awake
brightness; how the Josselyns grew cordial and confident
enough to confess that, with five little children in the

house, there was n't a great necessity for laying up against
a rainy day, and with stockings at a dollar and a half a
pair, one was apt to get the nine stitches, or a pretty
comfortable multiple of them, every Wednesday when the
wash came in ; and how these different kinds of lives,
coming together with a friendly friction, found themselves
not so uncongenial, or so incomprehensible to each other,
after all ; — all this, in its detail of bright words, I cannot
stop to tell you ; it would take a good many summers to
go through one like this so fully ; but when the big bell
rang for dinner, they all came down the ledge together,
and Sue and Martha Josselyn, for the first time in four
weeks, felt themselves fairly one with the current interest
and life of the gay house in which they had been dwellers
and yet only lookers-on.

Mrs. Thoresby, coming down to dinner, a few minutes
late, with her daughters, and pausing — as people always
did at the Green Cottage, without knowing why — to
step from the foot of the stairway to the open piazza-door,
and glance out before turning toward the dining-room,
saw the ledge party just dividing itself into its two little
streams, that were to head, respectively, for cottage and
hotel.

" It is a wonder to me that Mrs. Linceford allows it ! "
was her comment. " Just the odds and ends of all the
company here. And those girls, who might take whatever stand they pleased ! "

" Miss Leslie always finds out the nicest people, and
the best times, I think," said Etty, who had dragged
through but a dull morning behind the blinds of her
mother's window, puzzling over crochet, — which she

hated, because she said it was like everlastingly poking
one's finger after a sliver, — and had caught, now and
then, over the still air, the laughter and bird-notes that
came together from among the pines. One of the Miss
Haughtleys had sat with them ; but that only " stiffened
out the dulness," as Etty had declared, the instant the
young lady left them.

"Don't be pert, Etty. You don't know what you
want, or what is for your interest. The Haddens were
well enough, by themselves ; but when it comes to Tom,
Dick, and Harry ! "

"I don't believe that 's elegant, mamma," said Etty,
demurely ; "and there is n't Tom, Dick, nor Harry ;
only Dakie Thayne, and that nice, *nice* Miss Craydocke !
And — I *hate* the Haughtleys ! " This with a sudden
explosiveness at the last, after the demureness.

"Etty ! " and Mrs. Thoresby intoned an indescribable
astonishment of displeasure in her utterance of her daughter's name. "Remember yourself. You are neither to
be impertinent to me, nor to speak rudely of persons
whom I choose for your acquaintance. When you are
older, you will come to understand how these chance
meetings may lead to the most valuable friendships, or,
on the contrary, to the most mortifying embarrassments.
In the mean time, you are to be guided." After which
little sententious homily out of the Book of the World,
Mrs. Thoresby ruffled herself with dignity, and led her
brood away with her.

Next day, Tom, Dick, and Harry — that is to say,
Miss Craydocke, Susan and Martha Josselyn, and Leslie
Goldthwaite — were gathered in the first-named lady's

room, to make the great green curtain. And there Sin Saxon came in upon them, — ostensibly to bring the curtain-rings, and explain how she wanted them put on ; but after that she lingered.

"It 's like the Tower of Babel up stairs," she said, "and just about as likely ever to get built. I can't bear to stay where I can't hear myself talk. You 're nice and cosey here, Miss Craydocke." And, with that, she settled herself down on the floor, with all her little ruffles and flounces and billows of muslin heaping and curling themselves about her, till her pretty head and shoulders were like a new and charming sort of floating-island in the midst.

And it came to pass that presently the talk drifted round to vanities and vexations, — on this wise.

"Everybody wants to be everything," said Sin Saxon. "They don't say so, of course. But they keep objecting, and unsettling. Nothing hushes anybody up but proposing them for some especially magnificent part. And you can't hush them all at once in that way. If they 'd only say what they want, and be done with it ! But they 're so dreadfully polite ! Only finding out continual reasons why nobody will do for this and that, or have time to dress, or something, and waiting modestly to be suggested and shut up ! When I came down they were in full tilt about the Lady of Shalott. It 's to be one of the crack scenes, you know, — river of blue cambric, and a real, regular, lovely property-boat. Frank Scherman sent for it, and it came up on the stage yesterday, — drivers swearing all the way. Now they 'll go on for half an hour, at least ; and at the end of that time I shall

walk in — upon the plain of Shinar — with my hair all
let down, — it 's real, every *bit of it*, not a tail tied on
anywhere, — and tell them, I — myself — am to be the
Lady of Shalott ! I think I shall relish flinging in that
little bit of honesty, — like a dash of cold water into the
middle of a fry. Won't it sizzle ? "

She sat twirling the cord upon which the dozens of great
brass rings were strung, watching the shining ellipse they
made as they revolved, — like a child set down upon the
carpet with a plaything, — expecting no answer, only
waiting for the next vagrant whimsicality that should
come across her brain, — not altogether without method,
either, — to give it utterance.

" I don't suppose I could convince you of it," she resumed; " but I do actually have serious thoughts sometimes. I think that very likely some of us — most of
us — are going to the dogs. And I wonder what it will
be when we get there. Why don't you contradict — or
confirm — what I say, Miss Craydocke ? "

" You have n't said out, yet, have you ? "

Sin Saxon opened wide her great, wondering, saucy
blue eyes, and turned them full upon Miss Craydocke's
face. " Well, you *are* a oner! as somebody in Dickens
says. There 's no such thing as a leading question for
you. It 's like the rope the dog slipped his head out of,
and left the man holding fast at the other end, in touching confidence that he was coming on. I saw that once
on Broadway. Now I experience it. I suppose I 've
got to say more. Well, then, in a general way, do you
think living amounts to anything, Miss Craydocke ? "

" Whose living ? "

" Sharp — as a knife that 's just cut through a lemon !
Ours, then, if you please ; us girls', for instance."

" You have n't done much of your living yet, my dear."
The tone was gentle, as of one who looked down from such
a height of years that she felt tenderly the climbing that
had been, for those who had it yet to do.

" We 're as busy at it, too, as we can be. But sometimes I 've mistrusted something like what I discovered
very indignantly one day when I was four years old, and
fancied I was making a petticoat, sewing through and
through a bit of flannel. The thread had n't any knot
in it ! "

" That was very well, too, until you knew just where
to put the stitches that should stay."

" Which brings us to our subject of the morning, as the
sermons say sometimes, when they 're half through, or
ought to be. There are all kinds of stitches, — embroi-
dery, and plain over-and-over, and whippings, and darns !
When are we to make our knot and begin ? and which
kind are we to do ? "

" Most lives find occasion, more or less, for each. Prac-
tised fingers will know how to manage all."

" But — it 's — the — pro*por*tion ! " cried Sin, in a cre-
scendo that ended with an emphasis that was nearly a
little scream.

" I think that, when one looks to what is really needed
most and first, will arrange itself," said Miss Craydocke.
" Something gets crowded out, with us all. It depends
upon what, and how, and with what willingness we let it
go."

" *Now* we come to the superlative sort of people, — the

extra good ones, who let everything go that is n't solid
duty; all the ornament of life, — good looks, — tidiness
even, — and everything that 's the least bit jolly, and that
don't keep your high-mindedness on the strain.   I want
to be *low*-minded — *weak*-minded, at least, — now and
then.   I can't bear ferociously elevated people, who won't
say a word that don't count; people that talk about their
time being interrupted, (as if their time was n't everybody else's time, too,) because somebody comes in once
in a while for a friendly call; and who go about the streets
as if they were so intent upon some tremendous good work,
or big thinking, that it would be dangerous even to bow to
a common sinner, for fear of being waylaid and hindered.
I know people like that; and all I 've to say is, that, if
they 're to make up the heavenly circles, I 'd full as lief
go down lower, where they 're kind of social!"

There can scarcely be a subject touched, in ever so light
a way, — especially a moral or a spiritual subject, — in
however small a company of persons, that shall not set
in motion varied and intense currents of thought, — bear
diverse and searching application to consciousness and experience.   The Josselyns sat silent with the long breadths
of green cambric over their laps, listening with an amusement that freshened into their habitual work-day mood,
like a wilful little summer breeze born out of blue morning
skies, unconscious of clouds, to the oddities of Sin Saxon;
but the drift of her sayings, the meaning she actually had
under them, bore down upon their different knowledge
with a significance whose sharpness she had no dream of.
"Plain over-and-over," — how well it illustrated what
their young days and the disposal of them had been,

Miss Craydocke thought of the darns; her story cannot be told here; but she knew what it meant to have the darns of life fall to one's share, — to have the filling up to do, with dextrousness and pains and sacrifice, of holes that other people make!

For Leslie Goldthwaite she got the next word of the lesson she was learning, — "*It depends on what one is willing to let get crowded out.*"

Sin Saxon went on again.

" I 've had a special disgust given me to superiority. I would n't be superior for all the world. We had a superior specimen come among us at Highslope last year. She 's there yet, it 's commonly believed; but nobody takes the trouble to be positive of it. Reason why, she took up immediately such a position of mental and moral altitude above our heads, and became so sublimely uncon scious of all beneath, that all beneath was n't going to strain its neck to look after her, much less provide itself with telescopes. We 're pretty nice people, we think but we 're not particularly curious in astronomy. We heard great things of her, beforehand; and we were all ready to make much of her. We asked her to our parties. She came, with a look upon her as if some un- pleasant duty had forced her temporarily into purgatory. She shied round like a cat in a strange garret, as if all she wanted was to get out. She would n't dance; she would n't talk; she went home early, — to her studies, J suppose, and her plans for next day's unmitigated useful- ness. She took it for granted we had nothing in us *but* dance, and so — as Artemus Ward says — 'If the Ameri- can Eagle could solace itself in that way, we let it went!'

7 *

She might have done some good to us, — we needed to be done to, I don't doubt, — but it 's all over now. That light is under a bushel, and that city 's hid, so far as Highslope is concerned. And we 've pretty much made up our minds, among us, to be bad and jolly. Only sometimes I get thinking, — that 's all."

She got up, giving the string of rings a final whirl, and tossing them into Leslie Goldthwaite's lap. "Good by," she said, shaking down her flounces. "It 's time for me to go and assert myself at Shinar. '*Moi, c'est l'Empire!*' Napoleon was great when he said that. A great deal greater than if he 'd pretended to be meek, and want nothing but the public good!"

"What gets crowded out?" Day by day that is the great test of our life.

Just now, everything seemed likely to get crowded out with the young folks at Outledge, but dresses, characters, and rehearsals. The swivel the earth turned on at this moment was the coming Tuesday evening and its performance. And the central axis of that, to nearly every individual interest, was what such particular individual was to " be."

They had asked Leslie to take the part of Zorayda in the Three Moorish Princesses of the Alhambra. Jeannie and Elinor were to be Zayda and Zorahayda. As for Leslie, she liked well enough, as we know, to look pretty; it was, or had been, till other thoughts of late had begun to " crowd it out," something like a besetting weakness; she had only lately, to tell the whole truth as it seldom is told, begun to be ashamed, before her higher self, to turn, the first thing in the morning, with a certain half-mechanical anxiety, toward her glass, to see how she was looking. Without studying into separate causes of complexion and so forth, as older women given to these things come to do, she knew that somehow there was often a difference ; and beside the standing question in her mind as to whether there were a chance of her growing up to anything like positive beauty or not, there was apt often to be a reason why she would like *to-day*, if possible, to be in particular good looks.   When she got an invitation, or an excursion was planned, the first thing that came into her head was naturally what she should wear ; and a good deal of the pleasure would depend on that.   A party without an especially pretty dress did n't amount to much ; she could n't help that ; it did count with everybody, and it made a difference.   She would like, undoubtedly, a " pretty part " in these tableaux ; but there was more in Leslie Goldthwaite, even without touching upon the deep things, than all this.   *Only* a pretty part did not quite satisfy : she had capacity for something more.   In spite of the lovely Moorish costume to be contrived out of blue silk and white muslin, and to contrast so picturesquely with Jeannie's crimson, and the soft, snowy drapery of Elinor, she would have been half willing to be the " discreet Kadiga " instead ; for the old woman had really to look *something* as well as *somehow*, and there was a spirit and a fun in that.

The pros and cons and possibilities were working themselves gradually clear to her thoughts, as she sat and listened, with external attention in the beginning, to Sin Saxon's chatter.   Ideas about the adaptation of her dress-material, and the character she could bring out of, or get into, her part, mingled themselves together ; and Irving's delicious old legend that she had read hundreds of times, entranced, as a child, repeatea itself in snatches to her recollection. Jeannie must be stately; that would quite suit her. Elinor—must just be Elinor. Then the airs and graces remained for herself. She thought she could illustrate with some spirit the latent coquetry of the imprisoned beauty; she believed, notwithstanding the fashion in which the story measured out their speech in rations, — always an appropriate bit, and just so much of it to each, — that the gay Zorayda must have had the principal hand in their affairs, — must have put the others up to mischief, and coaxed most winningly the discreet Kadiga. She could make something out of it: it should n't be mere flat prettiness. She began to congratulate herself upon the character. And then her ingenious fancy flew off to something else that had occurred to her, and that she had only secretly proposed to Sin Saxon, — an illustration of a certain ancient nursery ballad, to vary by contrast the pathetic representations of Auld Robin Gray and the Lady of Shalott. It was a bright plan, and she was nearly sure she could carry it out; but it was not a "pretty part," and Sin Saxon had thought it fair she should have one; therefore Zorayda. All this was reason why Leslie's brain was busy, like her fingers, as she sat and sewed on the green curtain, and let Sin Saxon talk. Till Miss Craydocke said that, "Something always gets crowded out," and so those words came to her in the midst of all.

The Josselyns went away to their own room when the last rings had been sewn on; and the curtain was ready as had been promised, at ten o'clock. Leslie stayed, waiting for Dakie Thayne to come and fetch it. While she sat there, silent, by the window, Miss Craydocke brought out a new armful of something from a drawer, and came and placed her Shaker rocking-chair beside her. Leslie looked round, and saw her lap full of two little bright plaid dresses.

"It's only the button-holes," said Miss Craydocke. "I'm going to make them now, before they find me out."

Leslie looked very uncomprehending.

"You did n't suppose I let those girls come in here and spend their morning on that nonsense for nothing, did you? This is some of *their* work, — the work that's crowding all the frolic out of their lives. I've found out where they keep it, and I've stolen some. I'm Scotch, you know, and I believe in brownies. They're good to believe in. Old fables are generally *all but* true. You've only to 'put in one to make it so,' as children say in 'odd and even.'" And Miss Craydocke overcasted her first button-hole energetically.

Leslie Goldthwaite saw through the whole now, in a minute. "You did it on purpose, for an excuse!" she said; and there was a ring of applauding delight in her voice which a note of admiration poorly marks.

"Well, you must begin somehow," said Miss Craydocke. "And after you've once begun, you can keep on." Which, as a generality, was not so glittering, perhaps, as might be; but Leslie could imagine, with a warm heart-throb, what, in this case, Miss Craydocke's "keeping on" would be.

"I found them out by degrees," said Miss Craydocke. "They've been overhead here, this month nearly, and

if you *don't* listen nor look more than is ladylike, you
can't help scraps enough to piece something out of by that
time. They sit by their window, and I sit by mine. I
cough, and sneeze, and sing, as much as I find comfortable, and they can't help knowing where their neighbors
are ; and after that, it 's their look-out, of course. I lent
them some books one Sunday, and so we got on a sort of
visiting terms, and lately I 've gone in, sometimes, and
sat down awhile when I 've had an errand, and they 've
been here ; and the amount of it is, they 're two young
things that 'll grow old before they know they 've ever
been young, if somebody don't take hold. They 've
only got just so much time to stay; and if we don't contrive a holiday for them before it 's over, why, — there 's
the ' Inasmuch,' — that 's all."

Dakie Thayne came to the door to fetch Leslie and
the curtain.

" It 's all ready, Dakie, — here ; but I can't go just
now, or not unless they want me *very* much, and then
you 'll come, please, won't you, and let me know
again ? " said Leslie, bundling up the mass of cambric,
and piling it upon Dakie's arms.

Dakie looked disappointed, but promised, and departed.
They were finding him useful up stairs, and Leslie had
begged him to help.

" Now give me that other dress," she said, turning to
Miss Craydocke. " And you, — could n't you go and
steal something else ? " She spoke impetuously, and her
eyes shone with eagerness, and more.

" I 've had to lay a plan," resumed Miss Craydocke, as
Leslie took the measure of a button-hole and began.

" Change of work is as good as a rest. So I 've had them down here on the curtain among the girls. Next, I 'm going to have a bee. I 've got some things to finish up for Prissy Hoskins, and they 're likely to be wanted in something of a hurry. She 's got another aunt in Portsmouth, and if she can only be provided with proper things to wear, she can go down there, Aunt Hoskins says, and stay all winter, get some schooling, and see a city doctor. The man here tells them that something might be done for her hearing by a person skilled in such things, and Mrs. Hoskins says, ' There 's a little money of the child's own, from the vandoo when her father died,' that would pay for travelling and advice, and ' ef the right sort ain't to be had in Portsmouth, when she once gets started, she shall go whuzzever 't is, if she has to have a vandoo herself ! ' It 's a whole human life of comfort and usefulness, Leslie Goldthwaite, may be, that depends ! — Well, I 'll have a bee, and get Prissy fixed out. Her Portsmouth aunt is coming up, and will take her back. She 'll give her a welcome, but she 's poor herself, and can't afford much more. And then the Josselyns are to have a bee. Not everybody ; but you and me, and we 'll see by that time who else. It 's to begin as if we meant to have them all round, for the frolic and the sociability ; and besides that, we 'll steal all we can. For your part, you must get intimate. Nobody can do anything, except as a friend. And the last week they 're here is the very week I 'm going everywhere in ! I 'm going to charter the little red, and have parties of my own. We 'll have a picnic at the Cliff, and Prissy will wait on us with raspberries and cream.

We 'll walk up Feather-Cap, and ride up Giant's Cairn, and we 'll have a sunset at Minster Rock. And it 's going to be pleasant weather every day ! "

They stitched away, then, dropping their talk. Miss Craylocke was out of breath ; and Leslie measured her even loops with eyes that glittered more and more.

The half-dozen button-holes apiece were completed ; and then Miss Craydocke trotted off with the two little frocks upon her arm. She came back, bringing some two or three pairs of cotton-flannel drawers.

" I took them up, just as they lay, cut out and ready, on the bed. I would n't have a word. I told them I 'd nothing to do, and so I have n't. My hurry is coming on all of a sudden when I have my bee. Now I 've done it once, I can do it again. They 'll find out it 's my way, and when you 've once set up a way, people always turn out for it."

Miss Craydocke was in high glee.

Leslie stitched up three little legs before Dakie came again, and said they must have her up stairs.

One thing occurred to her, as they ran along the winding passages, up and down, and up again, to the new hall in the far-off L.

The Moorish dress would take so long to arrange. Would n't Imogen Thoresby like the part? She was only in the Three Fishers. Imogen and Jeannie met her as she came in.

" It is just you I wanted to find," cried Leslie, sealing her warm impulse with immediate act. " Will you be Zorayda, Imogen, — with Jeannie and Elinor, you know ? I 've got so much to do without. Sin Saxon

understands ; it 's a bit of a secret as yet.   I shall be *so*
obliged ! "

Imogen's blue eyes sparkled and widened.   It was just
what she had been secretly longing for.   But why in the
world should Leslie Goldthwaite want to give it up?

It had got crowded out, that was all.

Another thing kept coming into Leslie's head that day ;
— the yards of delicate grass-linen that she had hem-
stitched, and knotted into bands that summer, — just for
idle-work, when plain bindings and simple ruffling would
have done as well, — and all for her accumulating treasure of reserved robings, while here were these two girls
darning stockings, and sewing over heavy woollen stuffs,
that actual, inevitable work might be despatched in these
bright, warm hours that had been meant for holiday.   It
troubled her to think of it, seeing that the time was gone,
and nothing now but these threads and holes remained of
it to her share.

Martha Josselyn had asked her yesterday about the
stitch, — some little baby-daintiness she had thought of
for the mother who could n't afford embroideries and
thread-laces for her youngest and least of so many.   Leslie would go and show her, and, as Miss Craydocke said,
get intimate.   It was true there were certain little things
one could not do, except as a friend.

Meanwhile, Martha Josselyn must be the Sister of
Charity in that lovely tableau of Consolation.

It does not take long for two young girls to grow intimate over tableau plans and fancy stitches.   Two days
after this, Leslie Goldthwaite was as cosily established in
the Josselyns' room as if she had been there every day

all summer. Some people *are* like drops of quicksilver, as Martha Josselyn had declared, only one can't tell how that is till one gets out of the bottle.

"Thank you," she said to Leslie, as she mastered the little intricacy of the work upon the experimental scrap of cambric she had drawn. "I understand it now, I think, and I shall find time, somehow, after I get home, for what I want to do." With that, she laid it in a corner of her basket, and took up cotton-flannel again.

Leslie put something, twisted lightly in soft paper, beside it. "I want you to keep that, please, for a pattern, and to remember me," she said. "I 've made yards more than I really want. It 's nothing," she added, hastily interrupting the surprised and remonstrating thanks of the other. "And now we must see about that scapulary thing, or whatever it is, for your nun's dress."

And there was no more about it, only an unusual feeling in Martha Josselyn's heart, that came up warm long after, and by and by a little difference among Leslie Goldthwaite's pretty garnishings, where something had got crowded out.

This is the way, from small to great, things sort themselves.

"No man can serve two masters," is as full and true and strong upon the side of encouragement as of rebuke.

X.

THE tableaux had to be put off. Frank Scherman was obliged to go down to Boston, unexpectedly, to attend to business, and nothing could be done without him. The young girls felt all the reaction that comes with the sudden interruption of eager plans. A stagnation seemed to succeed to their excitement and energy. They were thrown back into a vacuum.

"There is nothing on earth to do, or to think about," said Florrie Arnall, dolefully.

"Just as much as there was last week," replied Josie Scherman, common-sense-ically. Frank was only her brother, and that made a difference. "There's Giant's Cairn as big as ever, and Feather-Cap, and Minster Rock, and the Spires. And there's plenty to do. Tableaux are n't everything. There's your 'howl,' Sin Saxon. That has n't come off yet."

"'It is n't the fall that hurts, — it's the fetch-up,' as the Irishman observed," said Sin Saxon, with a yawn. "It was n't that I doted particularly on the tableaux, but 'the waters wild went o'er my child, and I was left lamenting.' It was what I happened to be after at the moment. When I get ready for a go, I do hate to take off my bonnet and sit down at home."

"But the 'howl,' Sin! What's to become of that?"

"Ain't I howling all I can?"

And this was all Sin Saxon would say about it. The girls meant to keep her in mind, and to have their frolic,

—the half of them in the most imaginative ignorance as to what it might prove to be; but somehow their leader nerself seemed to have lost her enthusiasm or her intention.

Leslie Goldthwaite felt neither disappointment nor impatience. She had got a permanent interest. It is good always to have something to fall back upon. The tableaux would come by and by; meanwhile, there was plenty of time for their "bees," and for the Cliff.

They had long mornings in the pines, and cool, quiet afternoons in Miss Craydocke's pretty room. It was wonderful the cleverness the Josselyns had come to with little frocks. One a skirt, and the other a body, — they made nothing of finishing the whole at a sitting. "It's only seeing the end from the beginning," Martha said, when Leslie uttered her astonishment. "We know the way, right through; and no way seems long when you 've travelled it often." To be sure, Prissy Hoskins's delaines and calicoes did n't need to be contrived after Demorest's fashion-plates.

Then they had their holiday, taking the things over to the Cliff, and trying them all on Prissy, very much as if they had been a party of children, and she a paper doll. Her rosy little face and wilful curls came out of each prettier than the last, precisely as a paper dolly's does, and when at the end of all they got her into a bright violet print and a white bib-apron, it was well they were the last, for they could n't have had the heart to take her out of them. Leslie had made for her a small hoop, from the upper half of one of her own, and laced a little cover upon it, of striped seersucker, of which there was a

petticoat also to wear above. These, clear, clean, and
stiffened, came from Miss Craydocke's stores. She
never travelled without her charity-trunk, wherein —
put at once in perfect readiness for different use the moment they passed beyond her own — she kept all spare
material that waited for such call. Breadths of old
dresses, ripped and sponged and pressed, or starched,
ironed, and folded; flannel petticoats shrunken short;
stockings " cut down " in the old, thrifty, grandmother
fashion ; underclothing strongly patched (as she said, the
" Lord's mark put upon it, since it had pleased him to
give her the means to do without patches ") ; odds and
ends of bonnet-ribbons, dipped in spirits and rolled tightly
upon blocks, from which they unrolled nearly as good as
new ; — all these things, and more, religiously made the
most of for whomsoever they might first benefit, went
about with her in this, the biggest of her boxes, which,
give out from it as she might, she never seemed, she said,
to get quite to the bottom of.

Under the rounded skirts, below the short, plain trous-
ers, Prissy's ankles and feet were made shapely with
white stockings and new, stout boots. (Aunt Hoskins
believed in " white stockin's, or go athout. Bilin' an'
bleachin' an' comin' out new ; none o' yer aggravations 'v
everlastin' dirt-color.") And one thing more, the prettiest of all. A great net of golden-brown silk that Leslie
had begged Mrs. Linceford, who liked netting, to make,
gathered into strong, large meshes the unruly wealth of
hair brushed back in rippling lines from Prissy's temples,
and showing so its brighter, natural color from underneath, where the outside had grown sun-faded.

"I 'm just like Cinderella, — with four godmothers!" cried the child; and she danced up and down, as Leslie let her go from under her hands.

"You 're just like — a little heathen!" screamed Aunt Hoskins. "Where 's yer thanks?" Her own thanks spoke themselves, partly in an hysterical sort of chuckle and sniffle, that stopped each other short, and the rebuke with them. "But there! she don't know no better! 'T ain't fer every day, you need n't think. It 's for company to-day, an' fer Sundays, an' to go to Portsmouth."

"Don't spoil it for her, Mrs. Hoskins. Children hate to think it is n't for every day," said Leslie Goldthwaite.

But the child-antidote to that was also ready.

"I don't care," cried Prissy. "To-day 's a great, long day, and Sunday 's for ever and ever, and Portsmouth 'll be always."

"*Can't* yer stop ter kerchy, and say — Luddolight 'n massy, I donno what to *tell* ye ter say!" And Mrs. Hoskins sniffled and gurgled again, and gave it up.

"She has thanked us, I think," said Miss Craydocke, in her simple way, "when she called us God-mothers!" The word came home to her good heart. God had given her, the lonely woman, the larger motherhood. "Brothers, and sisters, and mothers!" She thought how Christ traced out the relationships, and claimed them even to himself!

"Now, for once, *you* 're to be done up. That 's general order number two," Miss Craydocke said to the Josselyn girls, as they all first met together again after the Cliff party. "We 've worked together till we 're friends. And so there 's not a word to be said. We

owe you time that we 've taken, and more that we mean
to take before you go.   I 'll tell you what for, when it 's
necessary."

It was a nicer matter to get the Josselyns to be helped
than to help.   It was not easy for them to bring forth
their breadths and their linings, and their braids that
were to be pieced, and their trimmings that were to be
turned, and to lay bare to other eyes all their little economies of contrivance ; but Miss Craydocke managed it by
simple straightforwardness, — by not behaving as if there
were anything to be glossed over or ignored.   Instead of
hushing up about economies, she brought them forward,
and gave them a most cheery and comfortable, not to say
dignified air.   It was all ordinary matter of course, —
the way everybody did, or ought to do.   This was the
freshest end of this breadth, and should go down ; this
other had a darn that might be cut across, and a straight
piecing made, for which the slope of the skirt would al
low, — *she* should do it so ; that hem might be taken off
altogether and a new one turned ; this was a very nice
trimming, and plenty of it, and the wrong side was
brighter than the right ; she knew a way of joining
worsted braid that never showed, — you might have a
dozen pieces in the binding of a skirt and not be noticed.
This little blue frock had no trimming ; they would finish
that at home.   No, the prettiest thing in the world for it
would be pipings of black silk, and Miss Craydocke had
some bits just right for covering cord, thick as a board,
big enough for nothing else ; and out they came, as did
many another thing, without remark, from her bags and
baskets.   She had hooks and eyes, and button-fasteners,

when these gave out; she used from her own cotton-
spools and skeins of silk; she had tailors' twist for button-holes, and large black cord for the pipings; and these
were but working implements, like scissors and thimble,
— taken for granted, without count.   There was nothing
on the surface for the most shrinking delicacy to rub
against; but there was a kindness that went down into
the hearts of the two young girls continually..

For an hour or two at least each day they sat together
so, for the being together.   The work was "taken up."
Dakie Thayne read stories to them sometimes; Miss
Craydocke had something always to produce and to sum-
mon them to sit and hear, — some sketch of strange adventure, or a ghost-marvel, or a bright, spicy magazine-
essay; or, knowing where to find sympathizers and
helpers, Dakie would rush in upon them uncalled, with
some discovery, or want, or beautiful thing to show of his
own.   They were quite a little coterie by themselves.
It shaped itself to this more and more.

Leslie did not neglect her own party.   She drove and
walked with Mrs. Linceford, and was ready for anything
the Haddens really wanted of her; but Mrs. Linceford
napped and lounged a good deal, and could spare her
then; and Jeannie and Elinor seemed somehow to feel
the want of her less than they had done, — Elinor unconsciously drawn away by new attraction, Jeannie
rather of a purpose.

I am afraid I cannot call it anything else but a little
loss of caste which seemed coming to Leslie Goldthwaite
just now, through these new intimacies of hers.   "Something always gets crowded out."   This, too, — her popu-

larity among the first, — might have to be, perhaps, one of the somethings.

Now and then she felt it so, — perceived the shade of difference toward her in the tone and manner of these young girls. I cannot say that it did not hurt her a little. She had self-love, of course ; yet, for all, she was loyal to the more generous love, — to the truer self-respect. If she could not have both, she would keep the best. There came to be a little pride in her own demeanor, — a waiting to be sought again.

" I can't think what has come over Les'," said Jeannie Hadden, one night, on the piazza, to a knot of girls. She spoke in a tone at once apologetic and annoyed. "She was always up to anything at home. I thought she meant to lead us all off here. She might have done almost what she pleased."

" Everybody likes Leslie," said Elinor.

" Why, yes, we all do," put in Mattie Shannon. " Only she will take up queer people, you see. And — well, they 're nice enough, I suppose ; only there 's never room enough for everybody."

" I thought we were all to be nowhere when she first came. There was something about her, — I don't know what, — not wonderful, but taking. 'Put her where you pleased, she was the central point of the picture,' Frank said." This came from Josie Scherman.

" And she 's just dropped all, to run after goodness knows what and whom ! I can't see through her ! " rejoined Jeannie, with a sort of finality in her accent that seemed to imply, " *I* wash my hands of her, and won't be supposed accountable."

8

"Knew ye not," broke in a gentle voice, "that she must be about her Master's business?" It was scarcely addressed to them. Miss Craydocke just breathed audibly the thought she could not help.

There came a downfall of silence upon the group.

When they took breath again, — "O, if she's *religious!*" Mattie Shannon just said, as of a thing yet farther off and more finally done with. And then their talk waited under a restraint again.

"I supposed we were all religious, — Sundays, at least," broke forth Sin Saxon suddenly, who, strangely, had not spoken before. "I don't know, though. Last Saturday night we danced the German till half past twelve, and we talked charades instead of going to church, till I felt — as if I'd sat all the morning with my feet over a register, reading a novel, when I'd ought to have been doing a German exercise or something. If she's religious every day, she's seven times better than we are, that's all. *I* think — she's got a knot to her thread!"

Nobody dared send Leslie Goldthwaite quite to Coventry after this.

Sin Saxon found herself in the position of many another leader, — obliged to make some demonstration to satisfy the aroused expectations of her followers. Her heart was no longer thoroughly in it; but she had promised them a "howl," and a howl they were determined upon, either with or against her.

Opportunity arose just now also. Madam Routh went off on a party to the Notch, with some New York friends, taking with her one or two of the younger pupils, for whom she felt most constant responsibility. The elder girls were domesticated and acquainted now at Outledge ; there were several matronly ladies with whom the whole party was sufficiently associated in daily intercourse for all the air of chaperonage that might be needed ; and one assistant pupil, whom, to be sure, the young ladies themselves counted as a most convenient nonentity, was left in nominal charge.

Now or never, the girls declared with one voice it must be. All they knew about it — the most of them — was that it was some sort of an out-of-hours frolic, such as boarding-school ne'er-do-weels delight in ; and it was to plague Miss Craydocke, against whom, by this time, they had none of them really any manner of spite ; neither had they any longer the idea of forcing her to evacuate ; but they had got wound up on that key at the beginning, and nobody thought of changing it. Nobody but Sin Saxon. She had begun, perhaps, to have a little feeling that she would change it, if she could.

Nevertheless, with such show of heartiness as she found possible, she assented to their demand, and the time was fixed. Her merry, mischievous temperament asserted itself as she went on, until she really grew into the mood for it once more, for the pure fun of the thing.

It took two days to get ready. After the German on Thursday night, the howl was announced to come off in Number Thirteen, West Wing. This, of course, was the boudoir ; but nobody but the initiated knew that. It was supposed to be Maud Walcott's room. The assistant pupil made faint remonstrances against she knew not what, and was politely told so ; moreover, she was pressingly invited to render herself with the other guests at the little piazza door, precisely at eleven. The matronly ladies, always amused, sometimes a little annoyed and scandalized at Sin Saxon's escapades, asked her, one and another, at different times, what it was all to be, and if she really thought she had better, and among themselves expressed tolerably grave doubts about proprieties, and wished Madam Routh would return. The vague mystery and excitement of the howl kept all the house gently agog for this Tuesday and Wednesday intervening. Sin Saxon gave out odd hints here and there in confidence.

It was to be a "spread"; and the "grub" (Sin was a boarding-school girl, you know, and had brothers in college) was to be all stolen. There was an uncommon clearance of cakes and doughnuts, and pie and cheese, from each meal, at this time. Cup-custards, even, disappeared, — cups and all. A cold supper, laid at nine on Wednesday evening, for some expected travellers, turned out a more meagre provision on the arrival of the guests than the good host of the Giant's Cairn had ever been known to make. At bedtime Sin Saxon presented herself in Miss Craydocke's room.

" There's something heavy on my conscience," she said, with a disquiet air. " I'm really worried; and it's too late to help it now."

Miss Craydocke looked at her with a kind anxiety. " It's never too late to *try* to help a mistake. And *you*, Miss Saxon, — you can always do what you choose."

She was afraid for her, — the good lady, — that her heedlessness might compromise herself and others in some untoward scrape. She did n't like these rumors of the

howl, — the last thing she thought of being her own rest
and comfort, which were to be purposely invaded.

"I've let the chance go by," said Sin Saxon, despe-
rately. "It's of no use now." And she rocked herself
back and forth in the Shaker chair, of which she had
taken possession.

"My dear," said Miss Craydocke, "if you would only
explain to me, — perhaps — "

"You *might!*" cried Sin, jumping up, and making a
rush at the good woman, seizing her by both hands.
"They'd never suspect you. It's that cold roast
chicken in the pantry. I *can't* get over it, that I did n't
take that!"

Sin was incorrigible. Miss Craydocke shook her head,
taking care to turn it aside at the same moment; for
she felt her lips twitch and her eyes twinkle, in spite of
herself.

"I won't take this till the time comes," said Sin, laying her hand on the back of the Shaker chair. "But
it's confiscated for to-morrow night, and I shall come for
it. And, Miss Craydocke, if you *do* manage about the
chicken, — I hate to trouble you to go down stairs, but I
dare say you want matches, or a drink of water, or
something, and another time I'll wait upon you with
pleasure, — here's the door, — made for the emergency,
— and I on the other side of it dissolved in tears of gratitude!"

And so, for the time, Sin Saxon disappeared.

The next afternoon, Jimmy Wigley brought a big basket of raspberries to the little piazza door. A pitcher
of cream vanished from the tea-table just before the gong

was struck. Nobody supposed the cat had got it. The people of the house understood pretty well what was going on, and who was at the bottom of it all; but Madam Routh's party was large, and the life of the place; they would wink hard and long before complaining at anything that might be done in the west wing.

Sin Saxon opened her door upon Miss Craydocke when she was dressed for the German, and about to go down stairs. "I 'll trust you," she said, "about the rocking-chair. You 'll want it, perhaps, till bedtime, and then you 'll just put it in here. I should n't like to disturb you by coming for it late. And please step in a minute now, won't you?"

She took her through the boudoir. There lay the "spread" upon a long table, contrived by the contribution of one ordinary little one from each sleeping-chamber, and covered by a pair of clean sheets, which swept the floor along the sides. About it were ranged chairs. Two pyramids of candles, built up ingeniously by the grouping of bedroom tins upon hidden supports, vine-sprays and mosses serving gracefully for concealment and decoration, stood, one on each side, half-way between the ends and centre. Cake-plates were garnished with wreathed oak-leaves; and in the midst a great white Indian basket held the red, piled-up berries, fresh and fragrant.

"That's the little bit of righteousness to save the city. That's paid for," said Sin Saxon. "Jimmy Wigley's gone home with more scrip than he ever got at once before; and if your chicken-heartedness had n't taken the wrong direction, Miss Craydocke, I should be perfectly at ease in my mind."

" It s very pretty," said Miss Craydocke ; " but do you think Madam Routh would quite approve ? And why could n't you have had it openly in the dining-room? And what do you call it a ' howl ' for ? " Miss Craydocke's questions came softly and hesitatingly, as her doubts came. The little festival was charming — but for the way and place.

" O Miss Craydocke ! Well, you 're not wicked, and you can't be supposed to know ; but you must take my word for it, that, if it was tamed down, the game would n't be worth the candle. And the howl? You just wait and see ! "

The invited guests were told to come to the little piazza door. The girls asked all their partners in the German, and the matronly ladies were asked, as a good many respectable people are civilly invited where their declining is counted upon. Leslie Goldthwaite, and the Haddens, and Mrs. Linceford, and the Thoresbys were all asked, and might come if they chose. Their stay would be another matter. And so the evening and the German went on.

Till eleven, when they broke up ; and the entertainers in a body rushed merrily and noisily along the passages to Number Thirteen, West Wing, rousing from their first naps many quietly disposed, delicate people, who kept early hours, and a few babies whose nurses and mammas would bear them anything but gratefully in mind through the midnight hours to come.

They gained two minutes, perhaps, upon their guests,

who had, some of them, to look up wraps, and to come round by the front hall and piazzas.   In these two minutes, by Sin Saxon's order, they seated themselves comfortably at table.   They had plenty of room ; but they spread their robes gracefully, — they had all dressed in their very prettiest to-night, — and they quite filled up the space.   Bright colors, and soft, rich textures floating and mingling together, were like a rainbow encircling the feast.   The candles had been touched with kerosene, and matches lay ready.   The lighting-up had been done in an instant. And then Sin Saxon went to the door, and drew back the chintz curtains from across the upper half, which was of glass.   A group of the guests, young men, were already there, beneath the elms outside.   But how should she see them, looking from the bright light into the tree-shadows ? She went quietly back, and took her place at the head, leaving the door fast bolted.

There came a knock.   Sin Saxon took no heed, but smilingly addressed herself to offering dainties right and left.   Some of the girls stared, and one or two half rose to go and give admittance.

" Keep your seats," said Sin, in her most ladylike way and tone, with the unchanged smile upon her face. "*That*'s the *howl!*"

They began to perceive the joke outside.   They began to knock vociferously.   They took up their cue with a readiness, and made plenty of noise; not doubting, as yet, that they should be admitted at last.   Some of the ladies came round, gave a glance, saw how things were going, and retreated ; — except a few, parties from other houses, who had escorts among the gentlemen, and who waited a

little to see how the frolic would end, or at least to re
claim their attendants.

Well, it was very unpardonable, — outrageous, the
scandalized neighbors were beginning already to say in
their rooms. Even Sin Saxon had a little excitement in
her eye beyond the fun, as she still maintained the most
graceful order within, and the exchange of courtesies
went on around the board, and the tumult increased with
out. They tree-toaded, they cat-called, they shouted, they
cheered, they howled, they even hissed. Sin Saxon sat
motionless an instant when it came to that, and gave a
glance toward the lights. A word from her would put
them out, and end the whole. She held her *coup* in .
reserve, however, knowing her resource, and sat, as it
were, with her finger on the spring, determined to carry
through coolly what she had begun.

Dakie Thayne had gone away with the Linceford party
when they crossed to the Green Cottage. Afterward,
he came out again and stood in the open road. Some
ladies, boarders at Blashford's, up above, came slowly
away from the uproar, homeward. One or two young
men detached themselves from the group on the piazza,
and followed to see them safe, as it belonged to them to
do. The rest sat themselves down, at this moment, upon
the steps and platform, and struck up, with one accord,
" We won't go home till morning." In the midst of this, a
part broke off and took up, discordantly, the refrain,
" Polly put the kettle on, we 'll all have tea " ; others
complicated the confusion further with " Cruel, cruel,
Polly Hopkins, treat me so — oh ! treat me so ! " Till
they fell, at last, into an indistinguishable jumble and

8*   L

clamor, from which extricated themselves now and again, and prevailed, the choruses of "Upidee," and "Bum-bum-bye," with an occasional drum-beat of emphasis given upon the door.

"Don't go back there, James," Dakie Thayne heard a voice from the retiring party say as they passed him, — "it's disgraceful!"

"The house won't hold Sin Saxon after this," said another. "They were out in the upper hall, half a dozen of them, just now, ringing their bells and calling for Mr. Biscombe."

"The poor man don't know who to side with. He don't want to lose the whole west wing. After all, there must be young people in the house, and if it were n't one thing it would be another. It's only a few fidgets that complain. They'll hush up and go off presently, and the whole thing will be a joke over the breakfast-table to-morrow morning, after everybody's had a little sleep."

The singing died partially away, just then, and some growling, less noisy, but more in earnest, began.

"They don't *mean* to let us in! I say, this is getting rather rough!"

"It's only to smash a pane of glass above the bolt, and let ourselves in. Why should n't we? We 're invited." The latent mob-element was very near developing itself in these young gentlemen, high-bred, but irate.

At this moment, a wagon came whirling down the road around the ledges. Dakie Thayne caught sight of the two white leaders, recognized them, and flew across to the hotel. "Stop!" cried he. At the same instant a figure moved hastily away from behind Miss Craydocke's blinds.

It was a mercy that the wagon had driven around to the front hall door.

A mercy in one way; but the misfortune was that the supper-party within knew nothing of it. A musical, lady-like laugh, quite in contrast to the demonstrative utterances outside, had just broken forth, in response to one of Sin Saxon's brightest speeches, when through the adjoining apartment came suddenly upon them the unlooked-for apparition of " the spinster." Miss Craydocke went straight across to the beleaguered door, drew the bolt, and threw it back. " Gently, young gentlemen! Draw up the piazza chairs, if you please, and sit down," said she. " Mr. Lowe, Mr. Brookhouse, here are plates; will you be kind enough to serve your friends?"

In three minutes she had filled and passed outward half a dozen saucers of fruit, and sent a basket of cake among them. Then she drew a seat for herself, and began to eat raspberries. It was all done so quickly — they were so entirely taken by surprise — that nobody, inside or out, gainsaid or delayed her by a word.

It was hardly done when a knock sounded at the door upon the passage. " Young ladies!" a voice called, — Madam Routh's.

She and her friends had driven down from the Notch by sunset and moonlight. Nobody had said anything to her of the disturbance when she came in; her arrival had rather stopped the complaints that had begun; for people are not malignant, after all, as a general thing, and there is a curious propensity in human nature which cools off indignation even at the greatest crimes, just as the culprit is likely to suffer. We are apt to check the foot just as we might have planted it upon the noxious creature, and to let off great state criminals on parole. Madam Routh had seen the bright light and the gathering about the west wing. She had caught some sounds of the commotion. She made her way at once to look after her charge.

Sin Saxon was not a pupil now, and there was no condign punishment actually to fear; but her heart stood still a second, for all that, and she realized that she had been on the verge of an "awful scrape." It was bad enough now, as Madam Routh stood there, gravely silent. She could not approve. She was amazed to see Miss Craydocke present, countenancing and matronizing. But Miss Craydocke *was* present, and it altered the whole face of affairs. Her eye took in, too, the modification of the room, — quite an elegant little private parlor as it had been made. The young men were gathered decorously about the doorway and upon the platform, one or two only politely assisting within. They had taken this cue as readily as the other; indeed, they were by no means aware that this was not the issue intended from the beginning, long as the joke had been allowed to go on, and their good-humor and courtesy had been instantly restored. Miss Craydocke, by one master-stroke of generous presence of mind, had achieved an instantaneous change in the position, and given an absolutely new complexion to the performance.

"It is late, young ladies," was all Madam Routh's remark at length.

"They gave up their German early on purpose; it was a little surprise they planned," Miss Craydocke said, as she moved to meet her.

And then Madam Routh, with wise, considerate dignity, took *her* cue. She even came forward to the table and accepted a little fruit; stayed five minutes, perhaps, and then, without a spoken word, her movement to go broke up, with unmistakable intent, the party. Fifteen minutes after, all was quiet in the west wing.

But Sin Saxon, when the doors closed at either hand, and the girls alone were left around the fragments of their feast, rushed impetuously across toward Miss Craydocke, and went down beside her on her knees.

" O you dear, magnificent old Christian ! " she cried out, and laid her head down on her lap, with little sobs, half laughter and half tears.

" There, there ! " — and Miss Craydocke softly patted her golden hair, and spoke as she would soothe a fretted and excited child.

Next morning, at breakfast, Sin Saxon was as beautifully ruffled, ratted, and crimped, — as gay, as bewitching, and defiant as ever, — seated next Madam Routh, assiduously devoted to her in the little attentions of the meal, in high spirits and favor; even saucily alluding, across the table, to " *our* howl, Miss Craydocke ! "

Public opinion was carried by storm ; the benison of sleep had laid wrath. Nobody knew that, an hour before, she had been in Madam Routh's room, making a clean breast of the whole transaction, and disclosing the truth of Miss Craydocke's magnanimous and tactful interposition, confessing that without this she had been at her wits' ends how to put a stop to it, and promising, like a sorry child, to behave better, and never do so any more.

Two hours later she came meekly to Miss Craydocke's

room, where the "bee" was gathered, — for mere companionship to-day, with chess and fancy-work, — her flourishes all laid aside, her very hair brushed close to her pretty head, and a plain gingham dress on.

"Miss Craydocke!" she said, with an air she could not divest of a little comicality, but with an earnestness behind it shining through her eyes, "I'm good; I'm converted. I want some tow-cloth to sew on immediately." And she sat down, folding her hands, waiting.

Miss Craydocke laughed. "I don't know. I'm afraid I have n't anything to be done just now, unless I cut out some very coarse, heavy homespun."

"I'd be glad if you would. Beggars must n't be choosers; but if they might, I should say it was the very thing. Sackcloth, you know; and then, perhaps, the ashes might be excused. I'm in solemn earnest, though. I'm reformed. You've done it; and you," she added, turning round short on Leslie Goldthwaite, — "you've been at it a long time, *unbeknownst* to yourself; and you, ma'am, — you finished it last night. It's been like the casting out of the devils in Scripture. They always give a howl, you know, and go out of 'em!"

XI.

SIN SAXON came heart and soul into Miss Craydocke's generous and delicate plans.   The work was
done, to be sure.   The third trunk, that had been "full
of old winter-dresses to be made over," was locked upon
the nice little completed frocks and sacks that forestalled
the care and hurry of " fall work" for the overburdened
mother, and should gladden her unexpecting eyes, as such
store only can gladden the anxious family manager who
feels the changeful, shortening days to come treading, with
their speedy demands, upon the very skirts of long, golden,
sunshiny August hours.

   Susan and Martha Josselyn felt, on their part, as only
busy workers feel who fasten the last thread, or dash a
period to the last page, and turn around to breathe the
breath of the free, and choose for once and for a while
what they shall do.   The first hour of this freedom rested
them more than the whole six weeks that they had been
getting half-rest, with the burden still upon their thought
and always waiting for their hands.   It was like the first
half-day to children, when school has closed and books are
brought home for the long vacation.   All the possible
delight of coming weeks is distilled to one delicious drop,
and tasted then.

   "It's 'none of my funeral,' I know," Sin Saxon said
to Miss Craydocke.   "I'm only an eleventh-hour helper;
but I'll come in for the holiday business, if you'll let me;
and perhaps, after all, that's more in my line."

Everything seemed to be in her line that she once took hold of. She had little private consultations with Miss Craydocke. "It's to be your party to Feather-Cap, but it shall be my party to Minster Rock," she said. "Leave that to me, please. Now the howl's off my hands, I feel equal to anything."

Just in time for the party to Minster Rock, a great basket and box from home arrived for Sin Saxon. In the first were delicious early peaches, rose-color and gold, wrapped one by one in soft paper and laid among fine sawdust; early pears also, with the summer incense in their spiciness; greenhouse grapes, white and amber and purple. The other held delicate cakes and confections unknown to Outledge, as carefully put up, and quite fresh and unharmed. "Everything comes in right for me," she exclaimed, running back and forth to Miss Craydocke with new and more charming discoveries as she excavated. Not a word did she say of the letter that had gone down from her four days before, asking her mother for these things, and to send her some money; "for a party," she told her, "that she would rather give here than to have her usual summer *fête* after her return."

"You quite eclipse and extinguish my poor little doings," said Miss Craydocke, admiring and rejoicing all the while as genuinely as Sin herself.

"Dear Miss Craydocke!" cried the girl, "if I thought it would seem like that, I would send and tip them all into the river. But you, — you *can't* be eclipsed! Your orbit runs too high above ours."

Sin Saxon's brightness and independence, that lapsed so easily into sauciness, and made it so hard for her to

observe the mere conventionalisms of respect, in no way
hindered the real reverence that grew in her toward the
superiority she recognized, and that now softened her tone
to a tenderness of humility before her friend.

There was a grace upon her in these days that all saw.
Over her real wit and native vivacity, it was like a por-
celain shade about a flame. One could look at it, and be
glad of it, without winking. The brightness was all there,
but there was a difference in the giving forth. What had
been a bit self-centred and self-conscious — bright as if
only for being bright and for dazzling — was outgoing and
self-forgetful, and so softened. Leslie Goldthwaite read
by it a new answer to some of her old questions. "What
harm is there in it?" she had asked herself on their first
meeting, when Sin Saxon's overflow of merry mischief,
that yet did "no special or obvious good," made her so
taking, — so the centre of whatever group into which she
came. Afterward, when, running to its height, this spirit
showed in behavior that raised misgivings among the scru-
pulous and orderly that would not let them any longer be
wholly amused, and came near betraying her, or actually
did betray her, into indecorums beyond excuse or countenance, Leslie had felt the harm, and begun to shrink away.
"Nothing *but* leaves" came back to her; her summer
thought recurred and drew to itself a new illustration.
This it was to have no aim but to rustle and flaunt; to grow
leaves continually; to make one's *self* central and conspic-
uous, and to fill great space. But now among these very
leaves gleamed something golden and glorious; something
was ripening suddenly out that had lain unseen in its
greenness; the time of figs seemed coming. Sin Saxon was

intent upon new purpose ; something to be *done* would not
let her "stand upon the order" or the fashion of her
doing. She forgot her little airs, that had been apt to
detract from her very wit, and leave it only smartness ;
bright things came to her, and she uttered and acted
them ; but they seemed involuntary and only on the way;
she could not help herself, and nobody would have had it
helped ; she was still Sin Saxon ; but she had simply told
the truth in her wayward way that morning. Miss Craydocke had done it, with her kindly patience that was no
stupidity, her simple dignity that never lowered itself and
that therefore could not be lowered, and her quiet con-
tinuance in generous well-doing, — and Sin Saxon was
different. She was won to a perception of the really best
in life, — that which this plain old spinster, with her
"scrap of lace and a front," had found worth living for
after the golden days were over. The impulse of temperament, and the generosity which made everything instant and entire with her, acted in this also, and carried her full over to an enthusiasm of affectionate co-
operation.

There were a few people at Outledge — of the sort who,
having once made up their minds that no good is ever to
come out of Nazareth, see all things in the light of that
conviction — who would not allow the praise of any volun-
tary amendment to this tempering and new direction of
Sin's vivacity. "It was time she was put down," they
said, "and they were glad that it was done. That last
outbreak had finished her. She might as well run after
people now, whom she had never noticed before : it was
plain there was nothing else left for her : her place was

gone, and her reign was over." Of all others, Mrs. Thoresby insisted upon this most strongly.

The whole school-party had considerably subsided. Madam Routh held a tighter rein; but that Sin Saxon had a place and a power still, she found ways to show in a new spirit. Into a quiet corner of the dancing-hall, — skimming her way, with the dance yet in her feet, between groups of staid observers, — she came straight, one evening, from a bright, spirited figure of the German, and stretched her hand to Martha Josselyn. "It's in your eyes," she whispered, — "come!"

Night after night Martha Josselyn had sat there, with the waltz-music in her ears, and her little feet, that had had one merry winter's training before the war, and many a home practice since with the younger ones, quivering to the time beneath her robes, and seen other girls chosen out and led away, — young matrons, and little short-petticoated children even, taken to "excursionize" between the figures, — while nobody thought of her. "I might be ninety, or a cripple," she said to her sister, "from their taking for granted it is nothing to me. How is it that everything goes by, and I only twenty?" There had been danger that Martha Josselyn's sweet, generous temper should get a dash of sour, only because of there lying alongside it a clear common-sense and a pure instinct of justice. Susan's heart longed with a motherly tenderness for her young sister when she said such words, — longed to put all pleasant things somehow within her reach. She had given it up for herself, years since. And now, all at once, Sin Saxon came and "took her out."

It was a more generous act than it shows for, written.

There is a little tacit consent about such things which few young people of a "set" have thought, desire, or courage to disregard.   Sin Saxon never did anything more gracefully.   It was one of the moments that came now, when she wist not that she shone.   She was dropping, little by little, in the reality of a better desire, that "satisfaction" Jeannie Hadden had spoken of, of "knowing when one is at one's prettiest," or doing one's cleverest.   The "leaf and the fruit" never fitted better in their significance than to Sin Saxon.   Something intenser and more truly living was taking the place of the mere flutter and flash and grace of effect.

It was the figure in which the dancers form in facing columns, two and two, the girls and the young men; when the "four hands round" keeps them moving in bright circles all along the floor, and under arches of raised and joined hands the girls came down, two and two, to the end, forming their long line face to face against the opposing line of their partners.   The German may be, in many respects, an undesirable dance ; it may be, as I have sometimes thought, at least a selfish dance, affording pleasure chiefly to the initiated few, and excluding gradually almost from society itself those who do not participate in it.   I speak of it here neither to uphold nor to condemn, — simply because they *did* dance it at Outledge as they do everywhere, and I cannot tell my story without it ; but I think at this moment, when Sin Saxon led the figure with Martha Josselyn, there was something lovely, not alone in its graceful grouping, but in the very spirit and possibility of the thing that so appeared.   There is scope and chance even here, young girls, for the beauty of kindness and generous thought. Even here, one may give a joy, may soothe a neglect, may make some heart conscious for a moment of the great warmth of a human welcome; and, though it be but to a pastime, I think it comes into the benison of the Master's words, when, even for this, some spirit gets a feeling like them, — " I was a stranger, and ye took me in."

Some one, standing behind where Leslie Goldthwaite came to her place at the end of the line by the hall-door, had followed and interpreted the whole ; had read the rare, shy pleasure in Martha Josselyn's face and movement, the bright, expressive warmth in Sin Saxon's, and the half-surprise of observation upon others ; and he thought as I do.

" ' Friends of the mammon of unrighteousness.'   That girl has even sanctified the German ! "

There was only one voice like that, — only one person who would so speak himself out. Leslie Goldthwaite turned quickly, and found herself face to face with Marmaduke Wharne. "I am so glad you have come ! " said she.

He regarded her shrewdly. " Then you can do without me," he said. " I did n't know by this time how it might be."

The last two had taken their places below Leslie while these words were exchanged, and now the whole line moved forward to meet their partners, and the waltz began. Frank Scherman had got back to-day, and was dancing with Sin Saxon. Leslie and Dakie Thayne were together, as they had been that first evening at Jefferson, and as they often were. The four stopped, after their merry whirl, in this same corner by the door where Mr.

Wharne was standing. Dakie Thayne shook hands with
his friend in his glad boy's way. Across their greetings
came Sin Saxon's words, spoken to her companion, —
" You 're to take her, Frank." · Frank Scherman was an
old childhood's friend, not a mere mountain acquaintance.
" I 'll bring up plenty of others first, but you 're to wait
and take *her*. And, wherever she got her training, you 'll
find she 's the featest-footed among us." It was among
the children — training them — that she had caught the
trick of it, but Sin Saxon did not know.

"I 'm ready to agree with you, with but just the
reservation that *you* could not make," Frank Scherman
answered.

"Nonsense," said Sin Saxon. " But stop! here 's
something better and quicker. They 're getting the bou-
quets. Give her yours. It 's your turn. Go ! "

Sin Saxon's blue eyes sparkled like two stars ; the
golden mist of her hair was tossed into lighter clouds by
exercise ; on her cheeks a bright rose-glow burned ; and
the lips parted with their sweetest, because most unconscious, curve over the tiny gleaming teeth. Her word
and her glance sent Frank Scherman straight to do her
bidding ; and a bunch of wild azalias and scarlet lilies was
laid in Martha Josselyn's hand, and she was taken out
again into the dance by the best partner there. We may
trust her to Sin Saxon and Frank Scherman, and her
own " feat-footedness " ; everything will not go by her
any more, and she but twenty.

Marmaduke Wharne watched it all with that keen
glance of his that was like a level line of fire from under
the rough, gray brows.

"I am glad you saw that," said Leslie Goldthwaite, watching also, and watching him.

"By the light of your own little text, — 'kind, and bright, and pleasant'?   You think it will do me good?"

"I think it *was* good; and I am glad you should really know Sin Saxon — at the first." And at the best; Marmaduke Wharne quite understood her. She gave him, unconsciously, the key to a whole character. It might as easily have been something quite different that he should have first seen in this young girl.

Next morning they all met on the piazza. Leslie Goldthwaite presented Sin Saxon to Mr. Wharne.

"So, my dear," he said, without preface, "you are the belle of the place?"

He looked to see how she would take it. There was not the first twinkle of a simper about eye or lip. Surprised, but quite gravely, she looked up, and met his odd bluntness with as quaint an honesty of her own. "I was pretty sure of it a while ago," she said. "And perhaps I was, in a demoralized sort of a way. But I 've come down, Mr. Wharne, — like the coon. I 'll tell you presently," she went on, — and she spoke now with warmth, — "who is the real belle, — the beautiful one of this place! There she comes!"

Miss Craydocke, in her nice, plain cambric morning-gown, and her smooth front, was approaching down the side-passage across the wing. Just as she had come one morning, weeks ago; and it was the identical "fresh petticoat" of that morning she wore now. The sudden coincidence and recollection struck Sin Saxon as she spoke. To her surprise, Miss Craydocke and Marmaduke Wharne

moved quickly toward each other, and grasped hands
like old friends.

"Then you know all about it!" Sin Saxon said, a few
minutes after, when she got her chance. "But you
don't know, sir," she added, with a desperate candor,
"the way I took to find it out! I've been tormenting
her, Mr. Wharne, all summer. And I'm heartily
ashamed of it."

Marmaduke Wharne smiled. There was something
about this girl that suited his own vein. "I doubt she
was tormented," he said, quietly.

At that Sin Saxon smiled too, and looked up out of
her hearty shame which she had truly felt upon her at
her own reminder. "No, Mr. Wharne, she never was;
but that was n't my fault. After all, perhaps, — is n't
that what the optimists think? — it was best so. I
should never have found her thoroughly out in any
other way. It's like" — and there she stopped short of
her comparison.

"Like what?" asked Mr. Wharne, waiting.

"I can't tell you now, sir," she answered with a gleam
of her old fearless brightness. "It's one end of a grand
idea, I believe, that I just touched on. I must think it
out, if I can, and see if it all holds together."

"And then I'm to have it?"

"It will take a monstrous deal of thinking, Mr.
Wharne."

"If I could only remember the chemicals!" said Sin
Saxon. She was down among the outcrops and fragments at the foot of Minster Rock. Close in around the

ones grew the short, mossy sward. In a safe hollow between two of them, against a back formed by another that rose higher with a smooth perpendicular, she had chosen her fireplace, and there she had been making the coffee. Quite intent upon the comfort of her friends she was to-day; something really to do she had; "in better business," as Leslie Goldthwaite phrased it to herself once, she found herself, than only to make herself brilliant and enchanting after the manner of the day at Feather-Cap. And let me assure you, if you have not tried it, that to make the coffee and arrange the feast at a picnic like this is something quite different from being merely an ornamental. There is the fire to coax with chips and twigs, and a good deal of smoke to swallow, and one's dress to disregard. And all the rest are off in scattered groups, not caring in the least to watch the pot boil, but supposing, none the less, that it will. To be sure, Frank Scherman and Dakie Thayne brought her firewood, and the water from the spring, and waited loyally while she seemed to need them; indeed, Frank Scherman, much as he unquestionably was charmed with her gay moods, stayed longest by her in her quiet ones; but she sent them off herself, at last, to climb with Leslie and the Josselyns again into the Minster, and see thence the wonderful picture that the late sloping light made on the far hills and fields that showed to their sight between framing tree-branches and tall trunk-shafts as they looked from out the dimness of the rock.

She sat there alone, working out a thought; and at last she spoke as I have said, — "If I could only remember the chemicals!"

" My dear! What do you mean? The chemicals?
For the coffee?" It was Miss Craydocke who ques-
tioned, coming up with Mr. Wharne.

"Not the coffee, — no," said Sin Saxon, laughing
rather absently, as too intent to be purely amused.
" But the — assaying. There, — I 've remembered *that*
word, at least ! "

Miss Craydocke was more than ever bewildered.
" What is it, my dear? An experiment? "

"No; an analogy. Something that's been in my
head these three days. I can't make everything quite
clear, Mr. Wharne, but I know it's there. I went, I
must tell you, a little while ago, to see some Colorado
specimens — ores and things — that some friends of ours
had, who are interested in the mines; and they talked
about the processes; and somebody explained. There
were gold and silver and iron and copper and lead and
sulphur, that had all been boiled up together some time,
and cooled into rock. And the thing was to sort them
out. First, they crushed the whole mass into powder,
and then did something to it — applied heat I believe —
to drive away the sulphur. That fumed off, and left the
rest as promiscuous as before. Then they — oxidized the
lead, however they managed it, and got that out. You
see I 'm not quite sure of the order of things, or of the
chemical part. But they got it out, and something took
it. Then they put in quicksilver, and that took hold of
the gold. Then there were silver and copper and iron.
So they had to put back the lead again, and that grap-
pled the silver. And what they did with the copper and
iron is just what I can't possibly recollect, but they di-

vided them somehow, and there was the great rock· rid-
dle all read out.   Now, have n't we been just like that
this summer?   And I wonder if the world is n't like it
somehow?   And ourselves, too, all muddled up, and not
knowing what we *are* made of, till the right chemicals
touch us?   There 's so much in it, Mr. Wharne, I
can't put it in clear order.   But it *is* there, — is n't it?"
   "Yes, it is there," answered Mr. Wharne, with the
briefest gravity.   For Miss Craydocke, there were little
shining drops standing in her eyes, and she tried not to
wink lest they should fall out, pretending they had been
really tears.   And what was there to cry about, you
know?
   "Here we have been," Sin Saxon resumed, "all
crushed up together, and the characters coming out little
by little, with different things.   Sulphur 's always the
first, — heats up and flies off, — it don't take long to find
that; and common oxygen gets at common lead; and so
on; but, dear Miss Craydocke, do you know what comforts me?   That you *must* have the quicksilver to dis-
cover the gold!"
   Miss Craydocke winked.   She had to do it then, and
the two little round drops fell.   They went down, unseen, into the short pasture-grass, and I wonder what
little wild-flowers grew of their watering some day afterward.
   It was getting a little too quiet between them now for
people on a picnic, perhaps; and so in a minute Sin Saxon said again: "It 's good to know there is a way to sort
everything out.   Perhaps the tares and wheat mean the
sam? thing.   Mr. Wharne, why is it that things seem

more sure and true as soon as we find out we can make
an allegory to them ? "

"Because we do *not* make the allegory. It is there as
you have said. 'I will open my mouth in parables. I
will utter things which have been kept secret from the
foundation of the world.' These things are that speech
of God that was in the beginning. The Word made
flesh, — it is he that interpreteth."

That was too great to give small answer to. Nobody
spoke again till Sin Saxon had to jump up to attend to her
coffee, that was boiling over, and then they took up their
little cares of the feast, and their chat over it.

Cakes and coffee, fruits and cream, — I do not care to
linger over these. I would rather take you to the cool,
shadowy, solemn Minster cavern, the deep, wondrous
recess in the face of solid rock, whose foundation and
whose roof are a mountain ; or above, upon the beetling
crag that makes but its porch-lintel, and looks forth itself
across great air-spaces toward its kindred cliffs, lesser and
more mighty, all around, making one listen in one's heart
for the awful voices wherein they call to each other for-
evermore.

The party had scattered again, after the repast, and
Leslie and the Josselyns had gone back into the Minster
entrance, where they never tired of standing, and out of
whose gloom now they looked upon all the flood of splendor, rosy, purple, and gold, which the royal sun flung
back — his last and richest largess — upon the heights
that looked longest after him. Mr. Wharne and Miss
Craydocke climbed the cliff. Sin Saxon, on her way up,
stopped short among the broken crags below. There was

something very earnest in her gaze, as she lifted her eyes, wide and beautiful with the wonder in them, to the face of granite upreared before her, and then turned slowly to look across and up the valley, where other and yet grander mountain ramparts thrust their great forbiddance on the reaching vision. She sat down, where she was, upon a rock.

" You are very tired ? " Frank Scherman said, inquir ingly.

" See how they measure themselves against each other," Sin Saxon said, for answer. " Look at them — Leslie and the rest — inside the Minster that arches up so many times their height above their heads, yet what a little bit — a mere mouse-hole — it is out of the cliff itself; and then look at the whole cliff against the Ledges, that, seen from anywhere else, seem to run so low along the river ; and compare the Ledges with Feather-Cap, and Feather-Cap with Giant's Cairn, and Giant's Cairn with Washington, thirty miles away ! "

" It is grand surveying," said Frank Scherman.

" I think we see things from the little best," rejoined Sin Saxon. " Washington is the big end of the tele-scope."

" Now you have made me look at it," said Frank Scherman, " I don't think I have been in any other spot that has given me such a real idea of the moun-tains as this. One must have steps to climb by, even in imagination. How impertinent we are, rushing at the tremendousness of Washington in the way we do ; scal-ing it in little pleasure-wagons, and never taking in the thought of it at all ! "

Something suddenly brought a flush to Sin Saxon's face, and almost a quiver to her lips. She was sitting with her hands clasped across her knees, and her head a little bent with a downward look, after that long, wondering mountain gaze, that had filled itself and then withdrawn for thought. She lifted her face suddenly to her companion. The impetuous look was in her eyes. " There's other measuring too, Frank. What a fool I 've been ! "

Frank Scherman was silent. It was a little awkward for him, scarcely comprehending what she meant. He could by no means agree with Sin Saxon when she called herself a fool ; yet he hardly knew what he was to contradict.

" We 're well placed at this minute. Leslie Goldthwaite and Dakie Thayne and the Josselyns half-way up above there, in the Minster. Mr. Wharne and Miss Craydocke at the top. And I down here, where I belong. Impertinence ! To think of the things I 've said in my silliness to that woman, whose greatness I can no more measure ! Why did n't somebody stop me ? I don't answer for you, Frank, and I won't keep you ; but I think I 'll just stay where I am, and not spoil the significance ! "

" I 'm content to rank beside you ; we can climb together," said Frank Scherman. " Even Miss Craydocke has not got to the highest, you see," he went on, a little hurriedly.

Sin Saxon broke in as hurriedly as he, with a deeper flush still upon her face. " There 's everything beyond. That 's part of it. But she helps one to feel what the higher — the Highest — must be. She 's like the rock she stands on. She 's one of the steps."

" Come, Asenath; let's go up." And he held out his
hand to her till she took it and rose. They had known
each other from childhood, as I said; but Frank Scherman
hardly ever called her by her name. "Miss Saxon" was
formal, and her school sobriquet he could not use. It
seemed to mean a great deal when he did say "Asenath."

And Sin Saxon took his hand and let him lead her up,
notwithstanding the "significance."

They are young, and I am not writing a love-story; but
I think they will "climb together"; and that the words
that wait to be said are mere words, — they have known
and understood each other so long.

" I feel like a camel at a fountain; drinking in what is
to last through the dry places," said Martha Josselyn, as
they came up. "Miss Saxon, you don't know what you
have given us to-day. I shall take home the hills in my
heart."

" We might have gone without seeing this," said Susan.

" No, you might n't," said Sin Saxon. " It's my good
luck to see you see it, that's all. It could n't be in the
order of things, you know, that you should be so near it,
and want it, and not have it, somehow."

" So much *is* in the order of things, though!" said
Martha. " And there are so many things we want, without knowing them even to *be!*"

" That's the beauty of it, I think," said Leslie Goldthwaite, turning back from where she stood, bright in the
sunset glory, on the open rock. Her voice was like that
of some young prophet of joy, she was so full of the gladness and loveliness of the time. " That's the beauty of

it, I think. There is such a worldful, and you never
know what you may be coming to next!' "

" Well, this is our last — of the mountains. We go on
Tuesday."

" It is n't your last of us, though, or of what we want
of you," rejoined Sin Saxon. " We must have the tableaux for Monday. We can't do without you in Robin
Gray or Consolation. And about Tuesday, — it 's only
your own making up of minds. You have n't written,
have you? They don't expect you? When a week 's
broken in upon, like a dollar, the rest is of no account.
And there 'll be sure to be something doing, so many are
going the week after."

" We shall have letters to-night," said Susan. " But I
think we must go on Tuesday."

Everybody had letters that night. The mail was in
early, and Captain Green came up from the post-office as
the Minster party was alighting from the wagons. He
gave Dakie Thayne the bag. It was Dakie's delight to
distribute, calling out the fortunate names as the expect-
ant group pressed around him, like people waiting the
issue of a lottery-venture.

" Mrs. Linceford, Miss Goldthwaite, Mrs. Linceford,
Mrs. *Lince*-ford! Master — hm! Thayne," and he pock-
eted a big one like a despatch. " Captain Jotham Green.
Where is he? Here, Captain Green; you and I have
got the biggest, if Mrs. Linceford does get the most. I
believe she tells her friends to write in bits, and put one
letter into three or four envelopes. When I was a *very*
little boy, I used to get a dollar changed into a hundred
coppers, and feel ever so much richer."

"That boy's forwardness is getting insufferable!" exclaimed Mrs. Thoresby, sitting apart, with two or three others, who had not joined the group about Dakie Thayne. "And why Captain Green should give *him* the bag always, I can't understand. It is growing to be a positive nuisance."

Nobody out of the Thoresby clique thought it so. They had a merry time together, — "you and I and the post," as Dakie said. But then, between you and me and that confidential personage, Mrs. Thoresby and her daughters had n't very many letters.

"That is all," said Dakie, shaking the bag. "They're only for the very good, to-night." He was not saucy: he was only brimming-over glad. He knew "Noll's" square handwriting, and his big envelopes.

There was great news to-night at the Cottage. They were to have a hero — perhaps two or three — among them. General Ingleside and friends were coming, early in the week, the Captain told them with expansive face. There are a great many generals and a great many heroes now. This man had been a hero beside Sheridan, and under Sherman. Colonel Ingleside he was at Stone River and Chattanooga, leading a brave Western regiment in desperate, magnificent charges, whose daring helped to turn that terrible point of the war and made his fame.

But Leslie, though her heart stirred at the thought of a real, great commander fresh from the field, had her own news that half neutralized the excitement of the other. Cousin Delight was coming, to share her room with her for the last fortnight.

9*

The Josselyns got their letters. Aunt Lucy was stay-ing on. Aunt Lucy's husband had gone away to preach for three Sundays for a parish where he had a prospect of a call. Mrs. Josselyn could not leave home imme-diately, therefore, although the girls should return ; and their room was the airiest for Aunt Lucy. There was no reason why they should not prolong their holiday if they chose, and they might hardly ever get away to the moun-tains again. More than all, Uncle David was off once more for China and Japan, and had given his sister two more fifties, — " for what did a sailor want of greenbacks after he got afloat ? " It was a " clover summer " for the Josselyns. Uncle David and his fifties would n't be back among them for two years or more. They must make the most of it.

Sin Saxon sat up late, writing this letter to her mother.

" DARLING MAMMA : —

" I 've just begun to find out really what to do here. Cream does n't always rise to the top. You remember the Josselyns, our quiet neighbors in town, that lived in the little house in the old-fashioned block opposite, — Sue Josselyn, Effie's schoolmate ? And how they used to tell me stories, and keep me to nursery-tea ? Well, they 're the cream, — they and Miss Craydocke. Sue has been in the hospitals, — two years, mamma ! — while I 've been learning nocturnes, and going to Germans. And Martha has been at home, sewing her face sharp ; and they 're here now to get rounded out. Well, now, mamma, I want so — a real dish of mountains and cream, if you ever heard of such a thing! I want to take a wagon, and invite a party as I did my little one to Minster Rock, and go through the hills, — be gone as many days as you will send me money for. And I want you to take the money from that particular little corner of your purse where my carpet and wall-paper and curtains, that were to newfurnish my room on my leaving school, are metaphorically rolled up. There's plenty there, you know; for you promised me my choice of everything, and I had fixed on that lovely pearl-gray paper at ——'s, with the ivy and holly pattern, and the ivy and scarlet-geranium carpet that was such a match. I'll have something cheaper, or nothing at all, and thank you unutterably, if you'll only let me have my way in this. It will do me so much good, mamma! More than you've the least idea of. People can do without French paper and Brussels carpets, but everybody has a right to mountain and sea and cloud glory, — only they don't half of them get it, and perhaps that's the other half's look-out!

"I know you'll understand me, mamma, particularly when I talk sense; for you always understood my nonsense when nobody else did. And I'm going to do your faith and discrimination credit yet.

"Your bad child, — with just a small, hidden savor of grace in her, *being* your child.

"ASENATH SAXON."

XII.

SATURDAY was a day of hammering, basting, draping, dressing, rehearsing, running from room to room. Up stairs, in Mrs. Green's garret, Leslie Goldthwaite and Dakie Thayne, with a third party never before introduced upon the stage, had a private practising; and at tea-time, when the great hall was cleared, they got up there with Sin Saxon and Frank Scherman, locked the doors, and in costume, with regular accompaniment of bell and curtain, the performance was repeated.

Dakie Thayne was stage-manager and curtain-puller; Sin Saxon and Frank Scherman represented audience, with clapping and stamping, and laughter that suspended both, — making as nearly the noise of two hundred as two could, — this being an essential part of the rehearsal in respect to the untried nerves of the *débutant*, which might easily be a little uncertain.

"He stands fire like a Yankee veteran."

"It's inimitable," said Sin Saxon, wiping the moist merriment from her eyes. "And your cap, Leslie! And that bonnet! And this unutterable old oddity of a gown! Who did contrive it all? and where did they come from? You'll carry off the glory of the evening. It ought to be the last."

"No, indeed," said Leslie. "Barbara Frietchie must be last, of course. But I'm so glad you think it will do. I hope they'll be amused."

"Amused! If you could only see your own face!"

"I see Sir Charles's, and that makes mine."

The new performer, you perceive, was an actor with a title.

That night's coach, driving up while the dress-rehearsal of the other tableaux was going on at the hall, brought Cousin Delight to the Green Cottage, and Leslie met her at the door.

Sunday morning was a pause and rest and hush of beauty and joy. They sat — Delight and Leslie — by their open window, where the smell of the lately harvested hay came over from the wide, sunshiny entrance of the great barn, and away beyond stretched the pine woods, and the hills swelled near in dusky evergreen, and indigo shadows, and lessened far down toward Winnipiseogee, to where, faint and tender and blue, the outline of little Ossipee peeped in between great shoulders so modestly, — seen only through the clearest air on days like this. Leslie's little table, with fresh white cover, held a vase of ferns and white convolvulus, and beside this Cousin Delight's two books that came out always from the top of her trunk, — her Bible and her little "Daily Food." To-day the verses from Old and New Testaments were these : — "The steps of a good man are ordered by the Lord, and he delighteth in his way." "Walk circumspectly, not as fools, but as wise, redeeming the time."

They had a talk about the first, — "The steps," — the little details, — not merely the general trend and final issue; if, indeed, these could be directed without the other.

"You always make me see things, Cousin Delight," Leslie said.

"It is very plain," Delight answered; "if people

only would read the Bible as they read even a careless
letter from a friend, counting each word of value, and
searching for more meaning and fresh inference to draw
out the most.   One word often answers great doubts and
askings that have troubled the world."

Afterward, they walked round by a still wood-path under the Ledge to the North Village, where there was a
service.   It was a plain little church, with unpainted
pews; but the windows looked forth upon a green moun-
tain-side, and whispers of oaks and pines and river-music
crept in, and the breath of sweet water-lilies, heaped in a
great bowl upon the communion-table of common stained
cherry-wood, floated up and filled the place.   The minister, a quiet, gray-haired man, stayed his foot an instant at
that simple altar, before he went up the few steps to the
desk.   He had a sermon in his pocket from the text,
"The hairs of your heads are all numbered."   He
changed it at the moment in his mind, and, when presently he rose to preach, gave forth, in a tone touched,
through the fresh presence of that reminding beauty,
with the very spontaneousness of the Master's own saying, — "Consider the lilies."   And then he told them of
God's momently thought and care.

There were scattered strangers, from various houses,
among the simple rural congregation.   Walking home
through the pines again, Delight and Leslie and Dakie
Thayne found themselves preceded and followed along
the narrow way.   Sin Saxon and Frank Scherman came
up and joined them when the wider openings permitted.

Two persons just in front were commenting upon the
sermon.

"Very fair for a country parson," said a tall, elegant-looking man, whose broad, intellectual brow was touched by dark hair slightly frosted, and whose lip had the curve that betokens self-reliance and strong decision, — "very fair. All the better for not flying too high. Narrow, of course. He seems to think the Almighty has nothing grander to do than to finger every little cog of the tremendous machinery of the universe, — that he measures out the ocean of his purposes as we drop a liquid from a phial. To me it seems belittling the Infinite."

" I don't know whether it is littleness or greatness, Robert, that must escape minutiæ," said his companion, apparently his wife. " If we could reach to the particles, perhaps we might move the mountains."

" We never agree upon this, Margie. We won't begin again. To my mind, the grand plan of things was settled ages ago, — the impulses generated that must needs work on. Foreknowledge and intention, doubtless: in that sense the hairs *were* numbered. But that there is a special direction and interference to-day for you and me — well, we won't argue, as I said; but I never can conceive it so; and I think a wider look at the world brings a question to all such primitive faith."

The speakers turned down a side-way with this, leaving the ledge path and their subject to our friends. Only to their thoughts at first; but presently Cousin Delight said, in a quiet tone, to Leslie, " That does n't account for the steps, does it ? "

"I am glad it *can't*," said Leslie.

Dakie Thayne turned a look toward Leslie, as if he would gladly know of what she spoke, — a look in which

a kind of gentle reverence was strangely mingled with
the open friendliness. I cannot easily indicate to you the
sort of feeling with which the boy had come to regard
this young girl, just above him in years and thought and
in the attitude which true womanhood, young or old,
takes toward man. He had no sisters ; he had been in-
timately.associated with no girl-companions ; he had lived
with his brother and an uncle and a young aunt, Rose.
Leslie Goldthwaite's kindness had drawn him into the
sphere of a new and powerful influence, — something different in thought and purpose from the apparent un-
thought about her ; and this lifted her up in his regard
and enshrined her with a sort of pure sanctity. He was
sometimes really timid before her, in the midst of his
frank chivalry.

"I wish you 'd tell me," he said suddenly, falling back
with her as the path narrowed again. "What are the
'steps'?"

"It was a verse we found this morning, — Cousin Delight and I," Leslie answered ; and as she spoke the color
came up full in her cheeks, and her voice was a little shy
and tremulous. "'The steps of a good man are ordered
by the Lord.' That one word seemed to make one certain. 'Steps,' — not path, nor the end of it ; but all the
way." Somehow she was quite out of breath as she
finished.

Meantime Sin Saxon and Frank had got with Miss
Goldthwaite, and were talking too.

"Set spinning," they heard Sin Saxon say, "and then
let go. That was his idea. Well ! Only it seems to me
there 's been especial pains taken to show us it can't be

done. Or else, why don't they find out perpetual motion? Everything stops after a while, unless — I can't talk theologically, but I mean all right — you hit it again."

"You 've a way of your own of putting things, Asenath," said Frank Scherman, — with a glance that beamed kindly and admiringly upon her and " her way,"—" but you 've put that clear to me as nobody else ever did. A proof set in the very laws themselves, — momentum that must lessen and lose itself with the square of the distance. The machinery cavil won't do."

" Wheels ; but a living spirit within the wheels," said Cousin Delight.

" Every instant a fresh impulse ; to think of it so makes it real, Miss Goldthwaite, — and grand and awful." The young man spoke with a strength in the clear voice that could be so light and gay.

"And tender, too. ' Thou layest Thine hand upon me,' " said Delight Goldthwaite.

Sin Saxon was quiet ; her own thought coming back upon her with a reflective force, and a thrill at her heart at Frank Scherman's words. Had these two only planned tableaux and danced Germans together before ?

Dakie Thayne walked on by Leslie Goldthwaite's side, in his happy content touched with something higher and brighter through that instant's approach and confidence. If I were to write down his thought as he walked, it would be with phrase and distinction peculiar to himself and to the boy-mind, — " It 's the real thing with her ; it don't make a fellow squirm like a pin put out at a caterpillar. She 's *good;* but she is n't *pious!* "

This was the Sunday that lay between the busy Satur day and Monday. "It is always so wherever Cousin Delight is," Leslie Goldthwaite said to herself, comparing it with other Sundays that had gone. Yet, she too, for weeks before, by the truth that had come into her own life and gone out from it, had been helping to make these moments possible. She had been shone upon, and had put forth ; henceforth she should scarcely know when the fruit was ripening or sowing itself anew, or the good and gladness of it were at human lips.

She was in Mrs. Linceford's room on Monday morning, putting high velvet-covered corks to the heels of her slippers, when Sin Saxon came over hurriedly, and tapped at the door.

" *Could* you be *two* old women ? " she asked, the in-stant Leslie opened. " Ginevra Thoresby has given out. She says it 's her cold, — that she does n't feel equal to it ; but the amount of it is, she got her chill with the Shannons going away so suddenly, and the Amy Robsart and Queen Elizabeth picture being dropped. There was nothing else to put her in, and so she won't be Bar-bara."

" Won't be Barbara Frietchie ! " cried Leslie, with an astonishment as if it had been angelhood refused.

" No. Barbara Frietchie is only an old woman in a cap and kerchief, and she just puts her head out of a window : the *flag* is the whole of it, Ginevra Thoresby says."

" *May* I do it ? Do you think I can be different enough in the two ? Will there be time ? " Leslie ques-tioned eagerly.

" We 'll change the programme, and put ' Taking the Oath' between. The caps can be different, and you can powder your hair for one, and — *would* it do to ask Miss Craydocke for a front for the other?" Sin Saxon had grown delicate in her feeling for the dear old friend whose hair had once been golden.

" I 'll tell her about it, and ask her to help me contrive. She 'll be sure to think of anything that can be thought of."

" Only there 's the dance afterward, and you had so much more costume for the other," Sin Saxon said, demurringly.

" Never mind. I shall *be* Barbara ; and Barbara would n't dance, I suppose."

" Mother Hubbard would, marvellously."

" Never mind," Leslie answered again, laying down the little slipper, finished.

" She don't care *what* she is, so that she helps along," Sin Saxon said of her, rejoining the others in the hall. " I 'm ashamed of myself and all the rest of you, beside her. Now make yourselves as fine as you please."

We must pass over the hours as only stories and dreams do, and put ourselves, at ten of the clock that night, behind the green curtain and the footlights, in the blaze of the three rows of bright lamps, that, one above another, poured their illumination from the left upon the stage, behind the wide picture-frame.

Susan Josselyn and Frank Scherman were just "posed" for "Consolation." They had given Susan this part, after all, because they wanted Martha for " Taking the Oath," afterward. Leslie Goldthwaite was giving a hasty touch to the tent drapery and the gray blanket; Leonard Brookhouse and Dakie Thayne manned the halyards for raising the curtain; there was the usual scuttling about the stage for hasty clearance; and Sin Saxon's hand was on the bell, when Grahame Lowe sprang hastily in through the dressing-room upon the scene.

"Hold on a minute," he said to Brookhouse. "Miss Saxon, General Ingleside and party are over at Green's, — been there since nine o'clock. Ought n't we to send compliments or something, before we finish up?"

Then there was a pressing forward and an excitement. The wounded soldier sprang from his couch; the nun came nearer, with a quick light in her eye; Leslie Goldthwaite, in her mob cap, quilted petticoat, big-flowered calico train, and high-heeled shoes; two or three supernumeraries, in Rebel gray, with bayonets, coming on in "Barbara Frietchie"; and Sir Charles, bouncing out from somewhere behind, to the great hazard of the frame of lights, — huddled together upon the stage and consulted. Dakie Thayne had dropped his cord and almost made a rush off at the first announcement; but he stood now, with a repressed eagerness that trembled through every fibre, and waited.

"Would he come?" "Is n't it too late?" "Would it be any compliment?" "Won't it be rude not to?" "All the patriotic pieces are just coming!" "Will the audience like to wait?" "Make a speech and tell 'em. You, Brookhouse." "O, he *must* come! Barbara Frietchie and the flag! Just think!" "Is n't it grand?" "O, I'm so frightened!" These were the hurried sentences that made the buzz behind the scenes; while in front " all the world wondered." Meanwhile, lamps trembled, the curtain vibrated, the very framework swayed.

" What is it? Fire?" queried a nervous voice from near the footlights

" This won't do," said Frank Scherman. " Speak to them, Brookhouse. Dakie Thayne, run over to Green's, and say, — The ladies' compliments to General Ingleside and friends, and beg the honor of their presence at the concluding tableaux."

Dakie was off with a glowing face. Something like an odd, knowing smile twinkling out from the glow also, as he looked up at Scherman and took his orders. All this while he had said nothing.

Leonard Brookhouse made his little speech, received with applause and a cheer. Then they quieted down behind the scenes, and a rustle and buzz began in front, — kept up for five minutes or so, in gentle fashion, till two gentlemen, in plain clothes, walked quietly in at the open door ; at sight of whom, with instinctive certainty, the whole assembly rose. Leslie Goldthwaite, peeping through the folds of the curtain, saw a tall, grand-looking man, in what may be called the youth of middle age, every inch a soldier, bowing as he was ushered forward to a seat vacated for him, and followed by one younger, who modestly ignored the notice intended for his chief. Dakie Thayne was making his way, with eyes alight and excited, down a side passage to his post.

Then the two actors hurried once more into position ; the stage was cleared by a whispered peremptory order ; the bell rung once, the tent trembling with some one whisking further out of sight behind it, — twice, and the curtain rose upon " Consolation."

Lovely as the picture is, it was lovelier in the living tableau.   There was something deep and intense in the
pale calm of Susan Josselyn's face, which they had not
counted on even when they discovered that hers was the
very face for the "Sister."   Something made you thrill
at the thought of what those eyes would show, if the downcast, quiet lids were raised.   The earnest gaze of the dy-
ing soldier met more, perhaps, in its uplifting ; for Frank
Scherman had a look, in this instant of enacting, that he
had never got before in all his practisings.   The picture
was too real for applause, — almost, it suddenly seemed,
for representation.

"Don't I know that face, Noll?"   General Ingleside
asked, in a low tone, of his companion.

Instead of answering at once, the younger man bent
further forward toward the stage, and his own very plain,
broad, honest face, full over against the downcast one of
the Sister of Mercy, took upon itself that force of magnetic
expression which makes a look felt even across a crowd
of other glances, as if there were but one straight line of
vision, and that between such two.   The curtain was going slowly down ; the veiling lids trembled, and the pale-
ness replaced itself with a slow-mounting flush of color
over the features, still held motionless.   They let the
cords run more quickly then.   She was getting tired,
they said ; the curtain had been up too long.   Be that as
it might, nothing could persuade Susan Josselyn to sit
again, and "Consolation" could not be repeated.

So then came "Mother Hubbard and her dog," — the
slow old lady and the knowing beast that was always getting one step ahead of her.   The possibility had occurred

to Leslie Goldthwaite as she and Dakie Thayne amused themselves one day with Captain Green's sagacious Sir Charles Grandison, a handsome black spaniel, whose trained accomplishment was to hold himself patiently in any posture in which he might be placed, until the word of release was given. You might stand him on his hind legs, with paws folded on his breast ; you might extend him on his back, with helpless legs in air ; you might put him in any attitude possible to be maintained, and maintain it he would, faithfully, until the signal was made. From this prompting came the Illustration of Mother Hubbard. Also, Leslie Goldthwaite had seized the hidden suggestion of application, and hinted it in certain touches of costume and order of performance. Nobody would think, perhaps, at first, that the striped scarlet and white petticoat under the tucked-up train, or the common print apron of dark blue, figured with innumerable little white stars, meant anything beyond the ordinary adjuncts of a traditional old woman's dress; but when, in the second scene, the bonnet went on, — an ancient marvel of exasperated front and crown, pitched over the forehead like an enormous helmet, and decorated, upon the side next the audience, with black and white eagle plumes springing straight up from the fastening of an American shield, — above all, when the dog himself appeared, " dressed in his clothes " (a cane, an all-round white collar and a natty little tie, a pair of three-dollar tasselled kid-gloves dangling from his left paw, and a small monitor hat with a big spread-eagle stuck above the brim, — the remaining details of costume being of no consequence), — when he stood " reading the news " from a

.nuge bulletin, — " LATEST BY CABLE FROM
EUROPE," — nobody could mistake the personification
of Old and Young America.

It had cost much pains and many dainty morsels, to
drill Sir Charles, with all the aid of his excellent funda-
mental education ; and the great fear had been that he
might fail them at the last. But the scenes were rapid,
in consideration of canine infirmity. If the cupboard was
empty, Mother Hubbard's basket behind was not ; he got
his morsels duly ; and the audience was " requested to
refrain from applause until the end." Refrain from
laughter they could not, as the idea dawned upon them
and developed ; but Sir Charles was used to that in the
execution of his ordinary tricks ; he could hardly have
done without it better than any other old actor. A dog
knows when he is having his day, to say nothing of doing
his duty ; and these things are as sustaining to him as to
anybody. This state of his mind, manifest in his air,
helped also to complete the Young America expression.
Mother Hubbard's mingled consternation and pride at
each successive achievement of her astonishing puppy
were inimitable. Each separate illustration made its
point. Patriotism, especially, came in when the under-
taker, bearing the pall with red-lettered border, — Rebel-
lion, — finds the dog, with upturned, knowing eye, and
parted jaws, suggestive as much of a good grip as of
laughter, half risen upon fore-paws, as far from " dead "
as ever, mounting guard over the old bone " Constitu-
tion."

The curtain fell at last, amid peals of applause and
calls for the actors.

Dakie Thayne had accompanied with the reading of the ballad, slightly transposed and adapted. As Leslie led Sir Charles before the curtain, in response to the continued demand, he added the concluding stanza, —

> " The dame made a courtesy,
> The dog made a bow ;
> The dame said, ' Your servant,'
> The dog said, ' Bow-wow.' "

Which, with a suppressed " Speak, sir ! " from Frank Scherman, was brought properly to pass. Done with cleverness and quickness from beginning to end, and taking the audience utterly by surprise, Leslie's little combination of wit and sagacity had been throughout a signal success. The actors crowded round her. " We 'd no idea of it ! " " Capital ! " " A great hit ! " they exclaimed. " Mother Hubbard is the star of the evening," said Leonard Brookhouse. " No, indeed," returned Leslie, patting Sir Charles's head, — " this is the dog-star." " Rather a Sirius reflection upon the rest of us," rejoined Brookhouse, shrugging his shoulders, as he walked off to take his place in the " Oath," and Leslie disappeared to make ready for " Barbara Frietchie."

Several persons, before and behind the curtain, were making up their minds, just now, to a fresh opinion. There was nothing so very slow or tame, after all, about Leslie Goldthwaite. Several others had known that long ago.

" Taking the Oath " was piquant and spirited. The touch of restive scorn that could come out on Martha Josselyn's face just suited her part ; and Leonard Bro⌐¹

house was very cool and courteous, and handsome and gentlemanly-triumphant as the Union officer.

"Barbara Frietchie" was grand. Grahame Lowe played Stonewall Jackson. They had improvised a pretty bit of scenery at the back, with a few sticks, some paint, brown carpet-paper, and a couple of mosquito-bars; — a Dutch gable with a lattice window, vines trained up over it, and bushes below. It was a moving tableau, enacted to the reading of Whittier's glorious ballad. "Only an old woman in a cap and kerchief, putting her head out at a garret window," — that was all; but the fire was in the young eyes under the painted wrinkles and the snowy hair; the arm stretched itself out quick and bravely at the very instant of the pistol-shot that startled timid ears; one skilful movement detached and seized the staff in its apparent fall, and the liberty-colors flashed full in Rebel faces, as the broken lower fragment went clattering to the stage. All depended on the one instant action and expression. These were perfect. The very spirit of Barbara stirred her representative. The curtain began to descend slowly, and the applause broke forth before the reading ended. But a hand, held up, hushed it till the concluding lines were given in thrilling tones, as the tableau was covered from sight.

> "Barbara Frietchie's work is o'er,
>   And the Rebel rides on his raids no more.
>
> "Honor to her! and let a tear
>   Fall, for her sake, on Stonewall's bier.
>
> "Over Barbara Frietchie's grave,
>   Flag of Freedom and Union, wave!

" Peace and order and beauty draw
Round thy symbol of light and law ;

" And ever the stars above look down
On thy stars below in Frederick town ! "

Then one great cheer broke forth, and was prolonged to three.

" Not be Barbara Frietchie ! " Leslie would not have missed that thrill for the finest beauty-part of all. For the applause — that was for the flag, of course, as Ginevra Thoresby said.

The benches were slid out at a window upon a lower roof, the curtain was looped up, and the footlights carried away ; the " music" came up, and took possession of the stage ; and the audience hall resolved itself into a ball-room. Under the chandelier, in the middle, a tableau not set forth in the programme was rehearsed and added a few minutes after.

Mrs. Thoresby, of course, had been introduced to the General ; Mrs. Thoresby, with her bright, full, gray curls and her handsome figure, stood holding him in conversation between introductions, graciously waiving her privilege as new-comers claimed their modest word. Mrs. Thoresby took possession ; had praised the tableaux, as " quite creditable, really, considering the resources we had," and was following a slight lead into a long talk, of information and advice on her part, about Dixville Notch The General thought he should go there, after a day or two at Outledge.

Just here came up Dakie Thayne. The actors, in costume, were gradually mingling among the audience,

and Barbara Frietchie, in white hair, from which there
was not time to remove the powder, plain cap and kerchief, and brown woollen gown, with her silken flag yet
in her hand, came with him. This boy, who "was always
everywhere," made no hesitation, but walked straight up
to the central group, taking Leslie by the hand. Close
to the General, he waited courteously for a long sentence
of Mrs. Thoresby's to be ended, and then said, simply,—
" Uncle James, this is my friend Miss Leslie Goldthwaite.
My brother, Dr. Ingleside — why, where is Noll ? "

Dr. Oliver Ingleside had stepped out of the circle in
the last half of the long sentence. The Sister of Mercy
— no longer in costume, however — had come down the
little flight of steps that led from the stage to the floor.
At their foot the young army surgeon was shaking hands
with Susan Josselyn. These two had had the chess-prac-
tice together — and other practice — down there among
the Southern hospitals.

Mrs. Thoresby's face was very like some fabric sub-
jected to chemical experiment, from which one color and
aspect has been suddenly and utterly discharged to make
room for something different and new. Between the
first and last there waits a blank. With this blank full
upon her, she stood there for one brief, unprecedented
instant in her life, a figure without presence or effect. I
have seen a daguerreotype in which were cap, hair, and
collar, quite correct, — what should have been a face
rubbed out. Mrs. Thoresby rubbed herself out, and so
performed her involuntary tableau.

" Of course I might have guessed. I wonder it never
occurred to me," Mrs. Linceford was replying, presently,

to her vacuous inquiry. "The name seemed familiar, too ; only he called himself 'Dakie.' I remember perfectly now. Old Jacob Thayne, the Chicago millionnaire. He married pretty little Mrs. Ingleside, the Illinois Representative's widow, that first winter I was in Washington. Why, Dakie must be a dollar prince ! "

He was just Dakie Thayne, though, for all that. He and Leslie and Cousin Delight, — the Josselyns and the Inglesides, — dear Miss Craydocke, hurrying up to congratulate, — Marmaduke Wharne looking on without a shade of cynicism in the gladness of his face, and Sin Saxon and Frank Scherman flitting up in the pauses of dance and promenade, — well, after all, these were the central group that night. The pivot of the little solar system was changed ; but the chief planets made but slight account of that ; they just felt that it had grown very warm and bright.

"O Chicken Little ! " Mrs. Linceford cried to Leslie Goldthwaite, giving her a small shake with her good-night kiss at her door. "How did you know the sky was going to fall ? And how have you led us all this chase to cheat Fox Lox at last ? "

But that was n't the way Chicken Little looked at it She did n't care much for the bit of dramatic *dénouement* that had come about by accident, — like a story, Elinor said, — or the touch of poetic justice that tickled Mrs. Linceford's world-instructed sense of fun. Dakie Thayne was n't a sum that needed proving. It was very nice that this famous general should be his uncle, — but not at all strange : they were just the sort of people he *must* belong to. And it was nicest of all that Dr. Ingleside and Susan Josselyn should have known each other, — "in the glory of their lives," she phrased it to herself, with a little flash of girl-enthusiasm and a vague suggestion of romance.

"Why did n't you tell us?" Mrs. Linceford said to Dakie Thayne next morning. "Everybody would have — " She stopped. She could not tell this boy to his frank face that everybody would have thought more and made more of him because his uncle had got brave stars on his shoulders, and his father had died leaving two millions or so of dollars.

"I know they would have," said Dakie Thayne. "That was just it. What is the use of telling things? I 'll wait till I 've done something that tells itself."

There was a pretty general break-up at Outledge during the week following. The tableaux were the *finale* of the season's gayety, — of this particular little episode, at least, which grew out of the association together of these personages of our story. There might come a later set, and later doings; but this last week of August sent the mere summer-birds fluttering. Madam Routh must be back in New York, to prepare for the reopening of her school; Mrs. Linceford had letters from her husband, proposing to meet her by the first, in N——, and so the Haddens would be off; the Thoresbys had stayed as long as they cared to in any one place where there seemed no special inducement; General Ingleside was going through the mountains to Dixville Notch. Rose Ingleside, — bright and charming as her name, — just a fit flower to put beside our Ladies' Delight, — finding out, at once, as all girls and women di l, her sweetness, and leaning more and more to the rare and delicate sphere of her quiet attraction, — Oliver and Dakie Thayne, — these were his family party; but there came to be question about Leslie and Delight. Would not they make six? And since Mrs. Linceford and her sisters must go, it seemed so exactly the thing for them to fall into; otherwise Miss Goldthwaite's journey hither would hardly seem to have been worth while. Early September was so lovely among the hills; opportunities for a party to Dixville Notch would not come every day; in short, Dakie had set his heart upon it, Rose begged, the General was as pressing as true politeness would allow, and it was settled.

"Only," Sin Saxon said, suddenly, on being told, "I should like if you would tell me, General Ingleside, the precise military expression synonymous with 'taking the wind out of one's sails.' Because that's just what you've done for me."

"My dear Miss Saxon! In what way?"

"Invited my party, — some of them, — and taken my road. That's all. I spoke first, though I didn't speak out loud. See here!" And she produced a letter from her mother, received that morning. "Observe the date, if you please, — August 24. 'Your letter reached me yesterday.' And it had travelled round, as usual, two days in papa's pocket, beside. I always allow for that. 'I quite approve your plan; provided, as you say, the party be properly matronized. I'—h'm—h'm!—That refers to little explanations of my own. Well, all is, I was going to do this very thing, — with enlargements. And now Miss Craydocke and I may collapse."

" Why ? when with you and your enlargements we might make the most admirable combination ? At least, the Dixville road is open to all."

" Very kind of you to say so, — the first part, I mean, — if you could possibly have helped it. But there are insurmountable obstacles on that Dixville road — to us. There 's a lion in the way. Don't you see we should be like the little ragged boys running after the soldier-company ? We could n't think of putting ourselves in that ' bony light,' especially before the eyes of Mrs. — Grundy." This last, as Mrs. Thoresby swept impressively along the piazza in full dinner costume.

" Unless you go first, and we run after you," suggested the General.

" All the same. You talked Dixville to her the very first evening, you know. No, nobody can have an original Dixville idea any more. And I 've been asking them, — the Josselyns, and Mr. Wharne and all, and was just coming to the Goldthwaites ; and now I 've got them on my hands, and I don't know where in the world to take them. That comes of keeping an inspiration to ripen. Well, it 's a lesson of wisdom ! Only, as Effie says about her housekeeping, the two dearest things in living are butter and experience ! "

Amidst laughter and banter and repartee, they came to it, of course ; the most delightful combination and joint arrangement. Two wagons, the General's and Dr. Ingleside's two saddle-horses, Frank Scherman's little mountain mare, that climbed like a cat, and was sure-footed as a chamois, — these with a side-saddle for the use of a lady sometimes upon the last, made up the general equipment of the expedition. All Mrs. Grundy knew was that they were wonderfully merry and excited together, until this plan came out as the upshot.

The Josselyns had not quite consented at once, though their faces were bright with a most thankful appreciation of the kindness that offered them such a pleasure ; nay, that entreated their companionship as a thing so genuinely coveted to make its own pleasure complete. Somehow, when the whole plan developed, there was a little sudden shrinking on Sue's part, perhaps on similar grounds to Sin Saxon's perception of insurmountable obstacles ; but she was shyer than Sin of putting forth her objections, and the general zeal and delight, and Martha's longing look, unconscious of cause why not, carried the day.

There had never been a blither setting off from the Giant's Cairn. All the remaining guests were gathered to see them go. There was not a mote in the blue air between Outledge and the crest of Washington. All the subtile strength of the hills — ores and sweet waters and resinous perfumes and breath of healing leaf and root distilled to absolute purity in the clear ether that only sweeps from such bare, thunder-scoured summits — made up the exhilarant draught in which they drank the mountain-joy and received afar off its baptism of delight.

It was beautiful to see the Josselyns so girlish and gay ; it was lovely to look at old Miss Craydocke, with her little tremors of pleasure, and the sudden glistenings in her eyes ; Sin Saxon's pretty face was clear and noble, with its pure impulse of kindliness, and her fun was like a sparkle upon deep waters. Dakie Thayne rushed about in a sort of general satisfaction which would not let him

10 *   o

be quiet anywhere. Outsiders looked with a kind of new, half-jealous respect on these privileged few who had so suddenly become the "General's party." Sin Saxon whispered to Leslie Goldthwaite, — "It 's neither his nor mine, honeysuckle ; it 's yours, — Henny-penny and all the rest of it, as Mrs. Linceford said." Leslie was glad with the crowning gladness of her bright summer.

"That girl has played her cards well," Mrs. Thoresby said of her, a little below her voice, as she saw the General himself making her especially comfortable with Cousin Delight in a back seat.

"Particularly, my dear madam," said Marmaduke Wharne, coming close and speaking with clear emphasis, "as she could not possibly have known that she had a trump in her hand !"

To tell of all that week's journeying, and of Dixville Notch, — the adventure, the brightness, tne beauty, and the glory, — the sympathy of abounding enjoyment, the waking of new life that it was to some of them, — the interchange of thought, the cementing of friendships, — would be to begin another story, possibly a yet longer one. Leslie's summer, according to the calendar, is already ended. Much in this world must pause unfinished, or come to abrupt conclusion. People " die suddenly at last," after the most tedious illnesses. " Married and lived happy ever after," is the inclusive summary that winds up many an old tale whose time of action only runs through hours. If in this summer-time with Leslie Gold thwaite your thoughts have broadened somewhat with

ners, some questions for you have been partly answered ;
if it has appeared to you how a life enriches itself by
drawing toward and going forth into the life of others
through seeing how this began with her, it is no unfinished tale that I leave with you.

A little picture I will give you, farther on, a hint of
something farther yet, and say good by.

Some of them came back to Outledge, and stayed far
into the still rich September. Delight and Leslie sat
before the Green Cottage one morning, in the heart of a
golden haze and a gorgeous bloom. All around the feet
of the great hills lay the garlands of early-ripened autumn.
You see nothing like it in the lowlands ; — nothing like
the fire of the maples, the carbuncle-splendor of the oaks,
the flash of scarlet sumachs and creepers, the illumination
of every kind of little leaf, in its own way, upon which
the frost-touch comes down from those tremendous heights
that stand rimy in each morning's sun, trying on white
caps that by and by they shall pull down heavily over
their brows, till they cloak all their shoulders also in the
like sculptured folds, to stand and wait, blind, awful
chrysalides, through the long winter of their death and
silence.

Delight and Leslie had got letters from the Josselyns
and Dakie Thayne. There was news in them such as
thrills always the half-comprehending sympathies of girlhood. Leslie's vague suggestion of romance had become
fulfilment. Dakie Thayne was wild with rejoicing that
dear old Noll was to marry Sue. "She had always made
him think of Noll, and his ways and likings, ever since
that day of the game of chess that by his means came to

grief. It was awful slang, but he could not help it: it was just the very jolliest go!"

Susan Josselyn's quiet letter said, — "That kindness which kept us on and made it beautiful for us, strangers, at Outledge, has brought to me, by God's providence, this great happiness of my life."

After a long pause of trying to take it in, Leslie looked up. "What a summer this has been! So full, — so much has happened! I feel as if I had been living such a great deal!"

"You have been living in others' lives. You have had a great deal to do with what has happened."

"O Cousin Delight! I have only been *among* it! I would not *do* — except such a very little."

"There is a working from us beyond our own. But if our working runs with that — ? You have done more than you will ever know, little one." Delight Gold-thwaite spoke very tenderly. Her own life, somehow, had been closely touched, through that which had grown and gathered about Leslie. "It depends on that abiding. 'In me, and I in you; so shall ye bear much fruit.'"

She stopped. She would not say more. Leslie thought her talking rather wide of the first suggestion; but this child would never know, as Delight had said, what a centre, in her simple, loving way, she had been for the working of a purpose beyond her thought.

Sin Saxon came across the lawn, crowned with gold and scarlet, trailing creepers twined about her shoulders, and flames of beauty in her full hands. "Miss Craydocke says she praised God with every leaf she took. I'm afraid I forgot to for the little ones. But I was so

greedy and so busy, getting them all for her. Come,
Miss Craydocke; we 've got no end of pressing to do, to
save half of them!"

"She can't do enough for her. O Cousin Delight,
the leaves *are* glorified, after all! Asenath never was
so charming; and she is more beautiful than ever!"

Delight's glance took in also another face than Asenath's, grown into something in these months that no
training or taking thought could have done for it.
"Yes," she said, in the same still way in which she had
spoken before, "that comes too, — as God wills. All
things shall be added."

My hint is of a Western home, just outside the leaping
growth and ceaseless stir of a great Western city; a large,
low, cosey mansion, with a certain Old-World mellowness
and rest in its aspect, — looking forth, even, as it does on
one side, upon the illimitable sunset-ward sweep of the
magnificent promise of the New; on the other, it catches
a glimpse, beyond and beside the town, of the calm blue
of a fresh-water ocean.

The place is "Ingleside"; the General will call it by
no other than the family name, — the sweet Scottish synonyme for Home-corner. And here, while I have been
writing and you reading these pages, he has had them all
with him; Oliver and Susan, on their bridal journey,
which waited for summer-time to come again, though
they have been six months married; Rose, of course, and
Dakie Thayne, home in vacation from a great school
where he is studying hard, hoping for West Point by
and by; Leslie Goldthwaite, who is Dakie's inspiration

still; and our Flower, our Pansie, our Delight,—golden-eyed Lady of innumerable sweet names.

The sweetest and truest of all, says the brave soldier and high-souled gentleman, is that which he has persuaded her to wear for life,—Delight Ingleside.

THE END

Cambridge : Stereotyped and Printed by Welch, Bigelow, & Co.

www.ingramcontent.com/pod-product-compliance
Lightning Source LLC
Chambersburg PA
CBHW020110030726
47498CB00006B/2030